FIFTEEN LOVE

FIFTEEN LOVE

NICOLE LEIGH SHEPHERD

a Pretty Tough novel

razor bill

An Imprint of Penguin Group (USA) Inc.

Fifteen Love

RAZORBILL

Published by the Penguin Group
Penguin Young Readers Group
345 Hudson Street, New York, New York 10014, U.S.A.
Penguin Group (USA) Inc., 375 Hudson Street,
New York, New York 10014, U.S.A.
Penguin Group (Canada), 90 Eglinton Avenue East, Suite 700,
Toronto, Ontario, Canada M4P 2Y3 (a division of Pearson Penguin Canada Inc.)
Penguin Books Ltd, 80 Strand, London WC2R 0RL, England
Penguin Ireland, 25 St Stephen's Green, Dublin 2, Ireland
(a division of Penguin Books Ltd)
Penguin Group (Australia), 250 Camberwell Road, Camberwell, Victoria 3124,
Australia (a division of Pearson Australia Group Pty Ltd)
Penguin Books India Pvt Ltd, 11 Community Centre,
Panchsheel Park, New Delhi – 110 017, India
Penguin Group (NZ), 67 Apollo Drive, Rosedale,
Auckland 0632, New Zealand (a division of Pearson New Zealand Ltd)
Penguin Books (South Africa) (Pty) Ltd, 24 Sturdee Avenue,
Rosebank, Johannesburg 2196, South Africa

Penguin Books Ltd, Registered Offices: 80 Strand, London WC2R 0RL, England

10 9 8 7 6 5 4 3 2 1

Copyright © 2012 PrettyTough Sports, LLC

ISBN 978-1-59514-418-8

Library of Congress Cataloging-in-Publication Data is available

Printed in the United States of America

To Mom and Dad

Chapter One
MAGGIE

"Hey, Bella, watch this!" I shout as I chase down her lob and return the tennis ball between my legs.

Thwack.

The ball hits the racquet's sweet spot and skims the top of the net. It spins across the mid-court and lands in front of my twin sister.

"Oh, yeah, back in the swing of things," I yell as I give a victory whoop.

Bella lets out a groan louder than the crashing Pacific Ocean waves behind the courts. "I knew I should have just used the ball machine!"

I'm too busy laughing at my sister's frustration to say anything.

She crosses her tan arms in front of her pale blue Nike dress, causing her racquet to slip out of her hand and kick up a bit of clay dust on the court. "Just my luck Joe had to leave this morning for New York. Wish I was going to the US Open."

"Oh, you know you miss playing tennis with your favorite sister." I spin the racquet grip between my palms like a whirligig, surprised that I'm having so much fun playing tennis today, considering how long it's been since I've played competitively.

"You're my *only* sister." Bella bends over and delicately picks up her racquet as a gentle breeze crinkles the palm fronds and whips her russet ponytail, a couple of stray pieces dancing in front her face. Strands of the same color tickle my nose too. I tuck them behind my ear.

Bella carefully brushes off her racquet, treating it more like a rare pink diamond than a grid of gut strings and composite. Then she remembers why we're here, and her brow furrows as she looks to me for an apology. "All I need is for you to help me prep for tomorrow, but you insist on messing around."

I don't apologize. Instead, I smile, knowing it will further irritate my twin.

And it does.

"You know how much this season means to me. And tryouts start tomorrow. *Tomorrow!*" Bella walks to the side of the court to switch her newest purple Head racquet for another one of her fourteen spares. She violently pushes more coffee-colored hair away from her face.

"Relax, Bellarina," I say. Bella danced until sixth grade, when my parents "encouraged" her to concentrate solely on one activity. But just because she stopped dancing doesn't mean I have to stop using my cleverest nickname for her.

Bella continues to yell. "Are you ever going to take anything seriously? I mean, we're freshman now, Maggie. About to start our high school career at Beachwood Academy, and all you ever want to do is clown around like we're still in kindergarten."

"When did high school become a career?" I grab a pair of fuzzy yellow tennis balls from the metal ball hopper behind me. Two club members carry beach bags along the wooden path adjacent to the tennis courts. We're practicing at the Beachwood Country Club, Malibu's mega exclusive beach oasis and the home of Bella's private coach, Joe Miller, or "Joe the Pro" as I've referred to him ever since I took tennis lessons with him when I was little. Even though Joe's off doing his Pro thing at a series of competitions, beginning with the US Open, Bella insisted on squeezing in some court time. And, to my own surprise, I said yes.

"You know what I mean. It's a big deal to start freshman year, and B-Dub's high school tennis program is practically famous."

I shake my head and attempt to juggle the two balls to tune out the sound of Bella's whining. I've always wanted to learn how to juggle—it's something I haven't done yet. I wonder where I could get lessons. Clown school maybe? Does B-Dub have a clowning team?

"And if I don't make the tennis team tomorrow, I might just . . . just . . . die." Bella adjusts her white and blue visor, ignoring the gawking of club members volleying on the court next to us. She's used to members making a big deal out of her since her trophies line the case outside the locker room to entice players to sign up for lessons with Joe.

I bounce one of the balls off the top of my hand and catch it before it hits the red clay. "Stop being so dramatic. You were part of the 'great' B-Dub middle school team and you're, like, nationally ranked or whatever. I think you can manage to make a high school tennis team." For a second, I catch myself wondering where I might have ended up in the rankings if I were still playing.

"I'm ranked eighty-first in the United States Tennis Association, SoCal Junior Division, Girls' U16. Which means there are eighty girls who are better than me in my age group alone." Bella huffs. "And four happen to be trying out for the varsity team at school tomorrow." She squats and begins swaying back and forth in what Joe refers to as the "ready position." "That's why this practice is so important."

Thoughts of my own ranking disappear as Bella spits out the digits of everyone she's ever encountered. I can't imagine caring about a silly number so much. "How do you sleep at night?" I ask then shake my head, wondering how we're possibly related, much less identical twins. I find my spot behind the baseline.

"Just serve, for real this time, okay?" Bella catches my eye and stares at me. It's almost like I'm looking in the mirror, except that I wouldn't be caught dead in that ridiculous tennis dress.

"I'm serious," Bella adds.

"When aren't you?"

"Very funny," she says, bouncing on the soles of her feet.

"Okay, sis. Watch this! Are you ready for another between-the-legs shot?" I bounce the yellow Penn ball in order to demonstrate, but really it's an attempt to divert Bella's attention away from my less-than-brilliant serve.

She glares at me from underneath her visor and continues to rock into her ready position. If she stares any harder, she'll burn a hole through my forehead.

I shake my head again and continue to bounce the ball off my hand, leg, and then wrist, wishing Bella could relax that all-work-and-no-play Anderson attitude she inherited from my parents. It's obvious Bella is happiest competing and showing off for Mom and Dad, but I wish we could have fun together, like we used to when we played doubles as kids. It's like now that I've retired from the life of the competitive tennis player, Bella and my parents barely have any use for me.

Not to mention, we would have so much more fun if she weren't such a stickler. I mean, she's never even agreed to switch places. What identical twins don't pretend that they're each other at least once? Especially when boys are involved.

"Maggie. Please!" she shouts like a stern teacher.

With a smile plastered across my face, I let the ball bounce and square the racquet. I widen my stance and strike the ball through my legs, using power from the movement of my hips. A quick wrist-snap upward produces a lob, and as I pivot back to ready position, I see a look of incredulity on Bella's face.

I used to love nailing trick shots on this very court. Back when my parents dressed Bella and me in matching tennis dresses and dropped us off for our private lessons with Joe. As usual, Bella was a total kiss-up. I, on the other hand, spent my time making miniature clay houses and climbing the fences that surrounded the courts, often attempting to somehow ruin my dress in the process, so I wouldn't have to wear it again.

The ball sails past my sister. Instead of lunging toward it, like she usually does, she stands there, points at the thick white line outlining the court, and simply says, "Out."

I'm having none of that. "Ace! I hit an ace! That was so in."

"It was so out!" Bella says. "And besides it wasn't even really a serve."

I break into my old victory dance. The same routine I used to bust out every time we won a match. "Oh yeah. Oh yeah. It's my birthday. It's my birthday," I sing, jutting my hips and swinging my racquet back and forth.

Bella giggles. "I haven't seen those moves in a long time."

"I've still got it," I chant. Really, though, if we're being technical about it, Bella is probably right—I've never *truly* aced the ball in my life.

"If you've still got it, then explain to me again why you don't play tennis anymore," Bella grumbles as she walks toward the net.

I point at her outfit and mime a little curtsy. "That's why."

"You know you love my look," Bella teases, pirouetting like the ballerina she once was.

I roll my eyes. "I'll never, ever wear a dress to play a sport. It's just not my style." I point my racquet at my brand-new Mongoose bike leaning against the fence. "That is."

"That"—Bella dismisses my beautiful bike with a flick of her hand—"is another hobby that you picked up on a whim because of some guy." Bella turns around and strolls back to her spot.

I stand frozen in place. Bella's words sting worse than a jellyfish. I'm not some pathetic clone who spends her days flitting from one activity to the next. Yeah, Ryan turned me on to BMX. Turns out boys just happen to like what I like, which is terribly convenient. "No," I call after her. "I choose to have fun. And boys have more fun."

"Sure," she mumbles loud enough so I can hear her. Then she

pirouettes a few more times while waiting for me to get back in the game. Her dress whirls around her.

"Whatever," I say, annoyed.

Behind the fence, Grace, Bella's friend from dance, walks the palm-tree lined path past the courts, spinning a set of keys around her index finger. A Capezio bag that she's clearly decided to adopt for beach-going purposes is slung across her shoulder, and a boogie board is tucked under her arm.

"Keep pirouetting like that and I'll drag your butt back to the dance studio myself," Grace shouts at Bella. She stops at the fence, leans her board against the navy chain link, and adjusts her flowered bikini top.

"Grace!" Bella screeches in the tone she usually saves for birthday surprises. She sprints toward her friend, leaving me alone on the court.

As Bella and Grace play catch-up, I stare at my racquet, a Wilson, left over from my tennis days. I attempt to spin the bottom of the grip on my palm like I used to, wishing I was airing on the half-pipe with my boyfriend Ryan and my new Mongoose bike instead of waiting for my sister to finish gabbing.

But I have to say, I actually enjoy being back out on the courts—the sound of the ball hitting the racquet's sweet spot is better than devouring an entire package of Skittles. I'll never admit that to Bella or my parents, though. They'd have a field day telling me about how I'm "my own worst enemy" and how it's "my own fault" that I'm "not as adept as Bella."

"Don't do that. You might drop it." Bella returns, seizing the racquet from my palm.

"What did Gracie have to say?" I ask, snatching the racquet back and walking to the ball hopper.

"The usual. She was filling me in about what's going on at the studio." Bella balances her racquet between her legs and gathers her poker-straight hair into a high pony.

"Do you miss it?" I ask.

"Miss what?" Bella snaps.

"Dance?"

"Not really. I love tennis," Bella retorts. "Can you believe Grace is going to be a junior?" she adds, changing the subject as quickly as she returns a serve. "And guess what?" She bounces on the balls of her feet and rises to her toes like she's wearing pointe shoes.

"What?" I ask as I begin twirling the racquet again.

"Grace is driving already. Isn't it awesome we know someone at Beachwood who drives?"

"Bells, we've been going to B-Dub since we were little. We probably know loads of people there who drive."

"Yeah, but Grace said if I ever needed a ride home, I could bum one off her."

"Great. And let me guess, she drives a . . ." I smirk and place my index finger to my chin like I'm deep in thought. "A Beemer."

Bella stops her little ballet routine and lets out a deep breath. "Just serve the ball, Maggie Mayhem." She uses the stupid nickname she christened me with after I broke Joe's nose at the last tournament I ever played.

"Oh, you want mayhem, huh?" I flip the ball into the air and smack it crosscourt. Bella gets to it this time, backhanding it to my

8

left. I run the ball down and use my powerful, nose-breaking forehand to hit the ball back to my sister.

Thwack.

"Ha!" I say. "Take that."

Bella sprints toward it, but she's too late. The ball hits the clay just inside the line, then pings into the back fence.

Bella stops dead in her tracks and places her hands on her hips, wearing the wide smile she always wears when she's on the court and in the zone. "I would *kill* for the spin and power you get with your forehand," she says, shaking her head like refusing to play tennis is some sort of terrible sin. "What a waste."

"I'm not *wasting* anything." I look over at my bike. "You should see the spin and power I can 'get,'" I air quote, "when I'm practicing tricks on the ramp. Ryan even said that—"

Bella interrupts me. "And what makes it worse is that you hardly try when you're playing tennis." She walks back to her spot behind the service line. "Think what you could be like if you actually gave it a teensy bit of effort."

"I try at what matters. For example, I'm trying really hard to get some air on the quarter pipe."

"And where's BMX going to get you? Or any of those things you end up not sticking with for more than a minute? Like soccer? Or surfing? Or what happened to painting and pottery, huh?"

I shrug. "I just didn't—"

"What about yoga? Whatever happened to your meditations? Oh, and what activity did that guy Greg do? Remember him? The one you hung out with last winter? Or did you forget about him already?" Bella adjusts her visor and straightens her shoulders like she's about to enter a pageant.

"Snowboarding," I mumble.

"Right. Snowboarding. You know, it's not like you can get a scholarship or win any money messing around with stuff that doesn't matter."

"Uh, not that I care about winning money or medals, but actually, yes, I can. Ever hear of the X Games? Or the Super Jam? How about the Olympics? They're adding more action sports events every year!" I roll my eyes. "But it's not about the fame and glory for me—it's about having fun."

"Tell me that you'd try all those extreme sports if it weren't for the guys."

I shake my head and look up in exasperation at the clear blue sky. "There are other reasons."

"Name one."

My face heats up. "Ugh . . . forget it. Let's just concentrate on playing. That's what you love so much isn't it?"

Bella stares at her racquet and straightens the strings with her fingers. Something she does when she's attempting to figure out what to say next. "I . . . I've worked my whole life for this. I'm very blessed to be able to play at the level I do."

"To the exclusion of everything else, right?"

When she looks up, the corners of her mouth crease, and I know then that I've hit on exactly what she's feeling. That's the thing about being twins. You can't hide anything from each other.

"Enough talk." Bella takes a deep breath and tosses the ball into the air. She whips her racquet like a machine. "Ehh!"

Thwack.

I lunge at the yellow blur as it bounces toward me, letting Bella have her moment of self-delusion. I forehand it toward her. "Take that!"

Thwack.

"Oh yeah?" She backhands the ball crosscourt. "How about that!"

I sprint toward it. Because I'm a lefty, it's an easy forehand return. "Is that all you've got?" I say, continuing the playful taunt.

Anticipating my return, Bella pulls back her racquet and slices it with a heavy topspin. "Check out that smoking shot!"

"Oh yeah? How about this one!"

Thwack.

We rally back and forth ten times before I yell, "Check this out!" Taking a wide step, I turn around and hit the ball between my legs. "And Maggie is back with another between-the-legs sista return!"

"Mags," Bella says through clenched teeth. Behind her, the ball sails in the direction of a woman who is making her way toward us.

It hits her right square on the side of the head. Whoopsies!

Immediately, Bella's face turns as red and tense as it did the day I broke a rail while grinding at the Colorado hotel we stayed at last spring for one of her tournaments.

When I garner enough courage to look at the woman I nailed, I see that she's rubbing the side of her head and wearing a collared shirt that reads *Beachwood Academy Tennis.*

If Bella's looks could kill, I'd be six feet under.

On the bright side, at least I didn't break her nose.

Chapter Two
BELLA

I cannot believe my sister embarrassed me like that. If we didn't look exactly alike, I'd swear we were switched at birth.

Maggie—with her ridiculous goofball return—has just pegged the tennis coach who will make or break my high school career right in the head.

I nervously glance at the coach, who's still rubbing her temple. I knew I shouldn't have asked Maggie to practice with me. She can never take anything seriously. Even when we were born, Maggie had to be pulled out a full fifteen minutes after me with forceps. My mom likes to joke that she was just having too much fun in the womb.

I take several tentative steps toward the coach and finally muster enough courage to ask, "Are you okay?"

But Olga Kasinski doesn't hear me. Instead, she shakes her head and composes herself. Then, she stares at my sister and me like I've seen her stare down her players' opposition at tournaments.

My sister attempts to ease the tension by lightly serving the ball—a new one—to me. Even though my first reaction is to nail it and then chastise Maggie for acting so recklessly, with the Beachwood Academy coach watching, I have no choice but to politely forehand the serve back to her. I don't want to be perceived as having an attitude problem.

Maggie and I smack the ball back and forth, falling into a familiar rhythm that reminds me of the short-lived days when we played together.

"Beautiful two-handed backhand." The legendary Coach Kasinski finally speaks, and to my relief she doesn't sound furious—or injured. "So smooth."

"Thanks," I say as my shoulders tighten up like new racquet strings. I bite my lip, breathe deeply like Joe taught me, and backhand another ball toward my sister. With a wicked topspin, the ball stops short, but Maggie somehow gets to it. She always does that, runs down every ball.

She powerfully carves the ball back to me, and like always, her natural forehand makes the ball bounce off the clay in a way that's tough to anticipate. But it's not enough to throw me off.

"And what a powerful forehand," Coach Kasinski says to Maggie. "From a lefty, no less." She nods knowingly, which stops me dead in my tracks for a moment and makes me miscalculate the ball's arc, sending an easy return Maggie's way. But, instead of smashing the ball like I know she's capable of, Maggie gently swats a lob back to me, purposely giving me the golden opportunity to smash it and end the game.

And I do. I smash it. Because this is *my* court, and I've worked really hard to kill it here. While Maggie was off having "fun," I've been putting every ounce of effort I possess into competing. Between the white lines is the only place I really feel at home—that is, when Maggie's not there, trying to bring me down by saying I'm too serious. She just doesn't get the importance of commitment, like I do, even though our parents have been trying to drill it into her for basically her entire life.

Maggie watches the ball hit the court beside her. She pretends to be scared of it.

I roll my eyes, knowing exactly what she's doing.

"And a decent smash," Coach Kasinski adds.

When Maggie turns around to grab another ball from the cart, I gaze in awe at Coach Kasinski. Not only was she an incredible tennis champ in her own regard, placing high in a number of Grand Slams (she never actually won a major but that's no big deal, considering her general amazingness), she's also coached more school championships than the Williams sisters have dollars. Plus, more of her former players have gone pro than those of any other high school coach I can think of.

She offers her hand to shake, and I accept before my mind recognizes what I'm doing. "I'm Olga Kasinski, coach of the twenty-time state championship Beachwood Academy Tennis Team," she says, her eyes filled with excitement. She's tanned and toned and, if it weren't for her dark hair, she'd look like Steffi Graf's clone.

"Hi, I'm—" But before I can finish, Coach Kasinski interjects.

"Bella Anderson, right?" she asks. Her black ponytail is pulled back so tight that you can almost feel the tension at her hairline. "It's so nice to finally meet you. You've been on my radar since USTA 12s."

My heart booms like a drum as I continue to shake Coach Kasinski's warm hand while staring into her ice-blue eyes. This is the moment I've been waiting for.

It's been almost 365 days since I found out that Coach Kasinski was behind the amazing O'Donnell sisters—both incredible players, and together, doubles champions. Once I heard that she was the coach who'd shaped Lauren and Minka's prestigious junior career, I was even more psyched to start high school. Rumor has it that once the girls go pro, a seven-figure endorsement deal is waiting for them. And it's all because they placed high in the best and most elite tournament around, the California Classic—well, that and an apparel company noticed their Anna Kournikova–like looks. It was Coach Kasinski who entered them into the Classic, which in turn paved the way for their future professional career. Clearly, this woman holds the golden key to tennis superstardom.

The legendary coach lets go of my hand.

"I saw you at the Memorial Day tournament in Colorado, and I have to say I was impressed with your backhand then. But to see it this close, it's fantastic. Your technique is strong and you have a lot of finesse."

"Thanks," I say, feeling my cheeks flush. I peek at Maggie, hoping she's hearing all this and that she notices how Coach Kasinski really gets my level of dedication. But she's too busy twirling the racquet some more.

"No, thank you for choosing Beachwood Academy. You're quite a talent, and I'm so glad you're going to be joining us at the high school level."

"Oh, of course—" I start to say.

Coach Kasinski cuts me off. "Not only do I think we have an excellent shot at another championship this year, but I feel that with both of you playing doubles"—Coach looks over at Maggie—"you might have a real shot at entering the California Classic. Like Minka and Lauren did last year."

I'm happily smiling in agreement, when it hits me what Coach just said. *What?* There is no way I heard her correctly.

Both of us? I glance at Maggie, who is now bouncing a tennis ball on her head, ignoring Coach Kasinski and me. "I'm sorry, what was that?" I ask her.

"There are a few wild card slots open every year. And every year a few of the Beachwood players earn a bid. Specifically, the players that I"—she places a hand on her chest—"feel stand out during the season. Meaning, of course, the players that work the hardest and play the Kasinski way."

Her words float aimlessly in my head without registering. I'm still too busy attempting to figure out what "both of you" meant. She must be referring to me and another player already on the Beachwood team. She couldn't have meant Maggie. There's no way a coach like Olga Kasinski would ever want my BMX-obsessed twin on the team. I mean, she's not blind. She has to see what Maggie's wearing at a country club: Vans, a black tank, jean shorts, and a Red Bull hat. Plus, we tried the tennis thing with Maggie. Even though she was pretty talented, she just clowned around the whole time. After the mess with Joe's nose, Maggie quit and never looked back.

"Speaking of Lauren and Minka, do you know them from local tournaments? They're a prime example of two sisters who really benefited from my training."

I tune back in to what the coach is saying. "Oh, uh, yeah. Yes. Of course I know Lauren and Minka," I say, attempting to impress her. Really though, I only know *of* them. Although I've certainly seen them around the tournaments, I've barely spoken a word to either of the sisters. They're older than me and normally just hang out by themselves.

"Yeah. They were good last year. But, from what I've seen this summer, it's possible they peaked a bit too early and have become complacent. That's why I'm always on the lookout for fresh talent." Coach Kasinski raises her eyebrows. "Like you and your sister." She walks toward Maggie, who at this point is attempting to simultaneously balance the butt cap on her palm and a ball on the top of her racquet. "It's so nice to meet you," Coach says. "I'm extremely impressed with your power and how you cover the court."

Oh no. Please don't talk to my sister.

The racquet falls off Maggie's palm and bops her on the head. She giggles and rubs the spot where the racquet hit her.

I jog next to Coach Kasinski, attempting to distract her. "Oh, my sister just helps me out every once in a while when I need someone to hit balls to me."

"That's nice." Coach turns to Maggie. "Hi, I'm Coach Olga Kasinski," she says, holding out her hand to my sister in the same way she did to me. "I'm with Beachwood Academy's tennis program."

"Hi," Maggie replies, her eyebrows raised in confusion. She shakes Coach's hand, glancing sideways at me.

"I knew about Bella, but I had no idea she had a twin sister with such incredible talent." By this point, Coach Kasinski's eyes are practically glimmering. "I'm so excited to meet you . . ." She waits for Maggie to introduce herself.

"Yeah. Nice to meet you too." Maggie pulls her hand back, her blue eyes bugging at me.

I shrug.

"What is your name? Where have you been hiding? Are you a natural lefty? And where did you learn that forehand? Does Joe Miller work with you too?"

Maggie looks at me again. "I uh . . . I'm Maggie, and I . . . uh . . ."

I can't stand it anymore, so I cut in. "Maggie played back in the day, but it didn't exactly go very well." I picture Joe's bruised and battered nose. "She's not really into tennis anymore."

Coach Kasinski ignores me, still staring at Maggie like she's a left-handed champion the likes of Monica or Martina. "It's obvious you're a tennis natural. With your angles, Maggie, and your sister's finesse and experience, you both seem uniquely equipped to make your mark on the tennis world."

"Uh . . ." I say, feeling shivers creep up my spine. My breath starts to come in gasping heaps. I was devastated when Maggie quit, but tennis is *my* thing now. I'm not a twin on the tennis court—I'm just Bella. And where else does that happen?

Coach Kasinski obviously doesn't notice that I'm hyperventilating because instead of stopping to see what it is that I'm trying to say, she continues talking. "You complement each other in such a special way. I'd really love to see how it translates on the doubles court." She places her hands on her hips and nods, as if hers is the final proclamation. Then she mutters, "Lauren and Minka certainly aren't setting the world on fire anymore. Maybe you two can get them in gear."

Wait. *Did I hear her right?* Lauren and Minka just placed tenth in doubles at the Governor's Cup.

Maggie's mouth drops. She looks at me in bewilderment.

"I hope the both of you will be at tryouts tomorrow. In fact, for the love of tennis, I'm making it mandatory that you both attend." She claps her hands quickly.

Mandatory?

"Uh. That's not possible," I say, pushing down the panic rising in my throat with each breath. I step in front of my sister. "We haven't played an actual match together in three years."

Coach Kasinski ignores me. "If what I've seen today is any indication, your competition doesn't stand a chance." Coach pauses, then looks at us victoriously. "That is, if you have my guidance."

Maggie swallows loudly. Hot tears press against the back of my eyes. *No. This can't be happening.* How could one of the greatest tennis coaches in the world think that Maggie is good enough to play at my level? Maggie quit. I didn't. I've been at this for ten straight years.

Coach's eyes are wide and excited. "Who knows? You might even be able to beat the O'Donnell sisters."

Did Coach Kasinski hit the Beachwood bar before the courts? I inch closer to her, hoping to smell whiskey or something to explain her delusions. Unfortunately, all I smell is sunscreen.

Maggie looks at me with dread in her eyes. She opens her mouth and squeaks, "No way . . ."

"Do you really think we could beat Minka and Lauren?" I step aside and cut my sister off, unable to resist asking.

"I do," Coach Kasinski says with sincerity. "And I have quite a knack at predicting these sorts of things. Maggie is quicker than Minka, and you, Bella, have a far better backhand than Lauren." Louder and more cheerfully, she finishes with, "If you work hard, I don't doubt you'll have lots of victories in your future."

I don't know if I'm more shocked that Coach Kasinski—*the* Coach Kasinski—thinks I have what it takes to beat Lauren and Minka and make it to the California Classic or that she thinks that Maggie will be the one to help me do it.

I look at Maggie in desperation, even though I know there's a fat chance she'll have the answers. She in turn looks at Coach and opens up her mouth to say something.

I jump in before she can. "Do you really think we could make enough of an impression during the regular season to play in the California Classic?"

"Wait. What?" Maggie grabs my shoulder.

"If you play the Kasinski way, I know you could."

I let out a deep breath. Participating in the California Classic is my chance to finally move up in the national ranks. A zillion images of my mom and dad comforting me all the other times I just missed out on making the cut flicker through my mind. Finally, I might be able to hold my head high when I pick up my racquet bag and head onto the court at one of the most important tournaments in all of junior tennis.

Coach Kasinski's apparently thinking along the same lines as me because she adds, "I can see the headlines now: 'Twins Double the Fun on the Court' and 'Anderson Sisters Double Down at the California Classic.'"

"No, you can't because . . ." Maggie begins to say until I nudge her, falling prey to the all-too-familiar images that have just hit my mental newsreel: me peeling my blood-splotched socks off my feet as I search for news articles about my performance, only to discover that there's no mention of Bella Anderson anywhere. Not on the web, or in the papers or magazines. Nowhere.

"And here I thought I was just stopping by to scout Bella. What a surprise. I'm so glad I discovered you today, Maggie. Tryouts are invitation only, so my running into you has definitely just made the difference. I see a great future for you two."

"We'll see you tomorrow," I reluctantly mutter, forcing myself to see the bigger picture. I wanted to do this without Maggie. The problem is, as I've been learning these last few years, being just Bella isn't good enough.

"What?" Maggie exclaims.

"Wonderful!" Coach Kasinski claps her hands sharply again, ignoring Maggie's confusion. "Rest up and I'll see you tomorrow after school."

"See you!" I call out to Coach as she disappears behind the palm trees.

Then Maggie stomps on my foot.

Chapter Three
MAGGIE

My sister has lost her mind.

Fat chance I'm ever stepping on the courts with her again, at least not competitively. Especially when I'm finally making progress on my bike. Bottom line: I am *not* spending the entire fall season hanging out with my stiff sister dressed in a white skirt or, ugh, even worse, one of those awful skort things. I'd rather eat that crazy-sounding squid dish my mom just ordered for dinner.

The relaxing jazz music at Beachwood Country Club's dimly lit restaurant, the Dolphin, irritates me, so I discreetly shove a white bud into my ear while my sister orders. Beyond the open terrace and glistening pool, the enormous setting sun casts an intense fuchsia glow over the ocean. I wish Ryan were here to witness the awesome sunset. I've left my bike out in the parking lot, so hopefully I can meet up with him later.

"Burger. Fries. Medium," I proudly announce to the waiter when he asks for my order. While Bella loves to nibble on lettuce leaves, I prefer real, non-rabbit food, like cheese steaks and onion rings at the fast-food joint on the pier. Of course, Miss Perfect refuses to ingest anything overly fatty or with too much sugar. She insists it makes her sluggish and messes with her game. But I'm the opposite. It's a good thing I don't conform to any stiff dietary rules because I've had my best days at the skate park after throwing back one of In-N-Out's big, greasy Double Double Animal Style burgers.

"So, are you girls ready for your first day of school?" my dad asks, turning his attention toward us after handing his leather-covered menu to the waiter. He's dressed in his typical starched collared shirt and beige tie.

I wait for Bella to answer since she's the one who's always clamoring to be the center of attention. Not that I care. It gives me more time to listen to my favorite band, Daydream.

But this time, Bella stays mum, focusing all her attention on straightening the fork and knife in front of her. I stare at her, wondering why she's not blabbing about signing me up . . . or at least about meeting the one and only Olga Kaniziwooshky or whatever her name is. Normally, Bella blurts out her latest accomplishments faster than I can say "pass the ketchup."

My dad looks at my mom. Mom gives him a smile as flat as her pressed suit. "Tomorrow's your very first day of high school." She moves a flickering candle to the side of the table. "You must be so excited."

Their asking us about our day instead of delving into a discussion of their latest litigation can mean only one thing: My parents are working on a case that involves a troubled teenager. Usually, our Tuesday night family dinner convo centers around recent affidavits, arbitrations, adjournments, and appeals at my parents' law firm. That is, unless my parents are working on something involving someone our age—then it's all eyes on us.

Still, Bella says nothing, and neither do I.

"Girls, we asked you a question," my mother prompts again after a long silence. She sips her blood-red wine.

I look at Bella, who sighs again.

"Can't wait," I finally say, before lifting the white tablecloth in front of my lap so I can tap on my iPhone's screen without their noticing.

"Yeah. Can't wait," my sister concurs flimsily. She repositions her water, and I see a look in her eyes that says she's waiting for my parents to ask her what's wrong.

Earlier, after Bella told that coach *we*'d try out as a doubles pair without even consulting me, I slammed down my racquet and demanded she get me out of this mess. (That is, after I already stomped on her foot.) But Bella, being stubborn and bullheaded (basically the same as me), crossed her arms and refused. She said, as much as she knew I didn't want to be on the courts with her again, this was her chance to be Coach's favorite player. And nothing comes between my sister and a goal.

After spewing some empty threats about how I would cover Bella's precious tennis clothes with grease from my bike if she didn't get me out of the tryouts, I stormed away and caught waves for about an hour by myself to release some steam.

Once I'd calmed down, guilt somehow wormed its way inside my freaky brain. Tennis does mean *everything* to my sister, and I admit I like hitting the ball around with her. So I went back to the court (where I knew she'd still be) and returned her serves in silence until dinner.

When we were done, I told her that if she wanted, I'd help her with her serves and slices and whatnot the rest of the time Joe was away, but that I wouldn't slap on some silly skort to play tennis again. My tennis days are like the Jonas Brothers and belly shirts—O-V-E-R.

My father clears his throat; the hard grumble suggests that he's had enough of our lack of cooperation. "When are tennis tryouts?" he asks, again attempting to get the conversation going.

"Yeah. When are tennis tryouts, Bells?" I nudge my sister.

"Tomorrow," Bella chirps. Then she looks down and begins spooning the ice cubes out of her water as part of her never-ending effort to avoid consuming anything too cold. (She claims that cold things make her cough, which in turn means her game suffers. It's, like, rule twenty-two on Bella's guide to a tennis-filled life, right after "thou shalt not have any fun.")

My mother smooths out her navy napkin across the white table-cloth. "And are you thinking of trying out for any interscholastic sports this fall, Maggie?" she asks in her courtroom voice.

Here it goes. Another Anderson assault on my latest extracur-ricular. They think I quit everything. They don't get that I look at life like a buffet—sports, boys, clubs, classes—all meant to be tasted. Why limit myself?

"Umm . . ." I glance at Bella before I answer. "Not in this lifetime."

She narrows her eyes at me. The unspoken tension between me and my sis is thicker than the steaming New England clam chowder that the waiter has just placed in front of my father.

"Well, Maggie Lynn, that's just unacceptable," Dad grunts. "How do you ever expect to make it in this world if you don't exert yourself now? Look at your sister. She's a model of the kind of perseverance we're talking about. Now, she could win a little more, but still, she's going to go places in life." He looks over at Bella approvingly, but his expression shifts once he catches sight of what she's *still* doing. "That is, if she shows the good sense to get her head out of her water." He turns to my sister—"Why are you so fixated by ice?"—then looks back at me. "And starts paying attention to her parents at the dinner table."

Bella's shoulders sink and she removes the spoon from her glass, the metal clinking against the last remaining ice cubes as she does so.

My mother places her hand on my dad's knee. "The girls are probably just anxious to start at Beachwood, Steven. You remember how nerve-wracking that can be. The beginning of high school." She lowers her voice to a whisper in what's either an attempt to distract him or an expression of an irrepressible urge to discuss work at all times. "How's that new divorce case coming? Are we making any headway?"

As my father begins to chat about his latest case, I blurt out, "Bella signed me up to play tennis at school."

My father looks like he just got smacked in the face. My mom's mouth hangs open like a nutcracker.

"What?" Dad finally says.

"Excuse me?" Mom shakes her head. "I thought we've been down this road already."

My father drops his spoon in his chowder. A few droplets splash onto the white tablecloth and onto his lap. My mother dabs at him with her napkin.

"Bella, why on earth would you . . ." Mom stops herself, clearing her throat as she rethinks her statement.

I pull the brim of the Red Bull hat that Ryan gave me for my birthday over my eyes. I can't deal with the parental inquisition.

"Does Joe know about this?" my father asks, reaching for his phone.

"Honey, wait a second," Mom says, placing a calming hand over my father's before he gets ahold of his cell. "If Maggie is integrated in the proper manner, I think it could actually be marvelous for the girls."

Dad eyes her suspiciously.

She continues regardless. "If Maggie and Bella played together again, they could strengthen that bond we're always talking about. That special twin bond."

My sister and I glance at each other disgustedly.

Since when does my mom say *marvelous*? And where did she dream up that Bella and me playing tennis together again is a good idea?

After a moment's hesitation, my father appears to concede. "Yes. It would be nice for the two of you to spend some quality time together." He eyes my mother warily, obviously still far from convinced.

Whoosh.

A fiery skillet appears beside our table, illuminating the dim room around us. We look up to see a waiter in a collared shirt and khaki shorts standing next to my mother, holding a dish that he's

27

just set on fire. "Saganaki?" he announces, though it comes out more like a question than anything.

"Yes. Thank you." My mother leans back as the waiter places the Greek flambéed "delicacy" in front of us.

There's nothing grosser than burnt cheese. Unless you count the grilled calamari my mom ordered for her entrée.

"So I'm assuming, Maggie, that you're on board with this," my dad says. He doesn't pause to let me answer. "I'm also assuming that you won't let this end in disaster like before." He leans back in his chair, confident that he's made his wishes known. Behind him, a waiter pulls out wooden chairs for what I'd call a clone couple—it's like seeing Barbie and Ken in the flesh. My dad must notice that my attention has shifted elsewhere because he adds, "If you're going to do this, you better be fully committed."

My mom nods in agreement.

"When is everybody going to let it go? I didn't mean to break Joe's nose." I glance beneath the tablecloth and select another track on my playlist, hoping the music will block the horrible memory . . . and my parents' chatter.

"Honey!" my mother raises her voice. "Please take that thing out of your ear when your father and I are speaking to you."

I pull out the earbud and wrap the wires around my iPhone.

"To continue," my dad says, "are you—as I just said—truly committed to playing tennis?"

I decide to play along. "Can I wear shorts?"

"See! That's exactly what I'm always talking about." Bella furiously slices the fried cheese in half. "She's not serious about anything."

"Calm down with the knife work there, psycho," I say, checking the time on my phone. "You're the one who signed me up."

Bella rolls her eyes at me. "No offense, Mags. But I just said yes to appease Coach. I would say yes to Coach if she asked me to lie on the court and make clay angels." She takes a tender bite, allowing no more than a tenth of an ounce into her mouth.

"Really, Bells? Was that the only reason?" I press on, my eyebrows raised.

"Yeah . . . uh-huh, of course," Bella answers quickly, shifting her eyes about uneasily. I must have struck a nerve

"Hold on, girls." My father raises his hand for us to stop. "Which coach are you talking about?"

My mother leans toward us as if proximity will help her better understand how her screwup daughter was recruited to play tennis.

Bella plays with her cheese, then looks up, an almost guilty expression on her face. "Coach Kasinski."

"Olga Kasinski?" my father gasps.

"*The* Olga Kasinski? Beachwood's head tennis coach wants *Maggie* to play?" my mother exclaims, her hand over her heart in shock.

While they're drooling over Olga, I sneak an earbud back into my ear and turn up my favorite Lil Wayne song so I can tune out my family again. I stare past the open terrace at the ocean and beyond, wondering if perhaps I should have saved myself the pain by telling them I wasn't planning to try out anyway, despite what Bella says.

"Maggie!" My mother interrupts my meditation.

I pull out the bud once more and shove my iPhone into the pocket of my Element hoodie.

"So let me get this straight," my dad begins, turning to my sister, his hands out in front of him, all serious and lawyerlike. "Olga Kasinski wants Maggie to join the team." A wrinkle appears between his brows as he processes this information. "She must have watched you two play today?"

"Yup," Bella answers, pushing the remaining cheese to the side of her plate. "She thinks Maggie has a powerful forehand, plus she loves her angles and the fact she's a lefty."

"She always did have a heck of a stroke," my mother says in a whisper, gazing past Bella. The glimmering lights above the bar create little white specks in the irises of her eyes.

"And you were just saying how you'd like to see Maggie participate in a team sport," Bella adds, earnestly.

I look over at her in surprise. Did she really just defend me? She's obviously just as shocked as I am that she said something supportive because she begins gulping down her water as if afraid of what else might come out of her mouth.

"Remember when Maggie played soccer?" my mother asks, wistfully.

"Of course. She scored eighteen goals in six games." My father's lips turn upward slightly in a hint of a smile, but then his expression shifts into a frown. "But then she quit." He looks at me directly. "What worries me is that we crossed this bridge a long time ago and it didn't go well. And this time it's Bella's future that you're putting at risk."

Bella opens her mouth to speak, but my dad cuts her off before she can. "Even if your sister," he nods at Bella, "thinks this is a good idea"—Bella's cheeks flush at that one—"and even though we certainly want you to participate in a school-sanctioned sport, I'm concerned about your involvement being something that directly impacts your sister."

Heat courses through my body. "Why?! Why are you so worried about me screwing everything up for your perfect, darling Bella?"

"That's not it, sweetie," my mom says. The words come out calmly but in that moment I feel like she's turning on me as well. "It's just you know how hard your sister works."

Bella looks down at her food as if she's ashamed, but I know it's just an act—I can see the pride in her eyes.

Mom glances at her, then adds, "There's a lot at stake for Bella."

"And, as exciting as this all sounds, we can't let her success be limited by your problems with prioritization," my dad concludes, severely.

"Ughh . . . why do you all always think that I have 'problems with prioritization'?" I say the last part in a mocking tone. "If you'd just give me a chance, I'd show you that—"

Dad cuts me off. "We gave you a chance, and you ended up hitting Joe in the nose."

"Seriously? That again? Twice in one dinner conversation? Will you guys just let it go? It was *an accident*," I insist, practically whining.

"An accident that was caused by your decision to attend a party instead of practice like your sister," Dad says, pursing his lips.

I stare at him, shooting daggers with my eyes. He's right that the day before my last big match I chose to attend my best bud's birthday party, instead of practicing like Bella did. But what he forgot to mention is how when I double faulted five times, he and my mom got up and left to go watch Bella *practice*. Once I noticed they were gone, I lost my temper and pegged a ball toward the bench, which unfortunately was right where Joe was standing.

"That party cost you tennis," Dad says, pursing his lips.

You picking Bella over me is what really cost me tennis.

I forcefully tear a piece of bread off the crusty loaf, imagining myself completing a double peg stall. Why focus on one sport anyway when I can try them all? I'm only fifteen.

Bella sucks in a deep breath as if gathering her strength. "Coach Kasinski thinks Maggie and I would make an excellent doubles team. She said we complement each other and might be even better than Lauren and Minka O'Donnell."

My mother gasps.

My father drops his spoon, splashing more soup everywhere.

Bella, meanwhile, adjusts her headband, as if that'll bring everything back to normal.

I stare at my sister in disbelief. She's *really* going for it. Our family's arguments have always been carried out like we're in a courtroom, and Bella can play my parents' games with the best of them.

Once my mom regains her composure, she says, "Well, I have to agree. There's a lot of potential there. The both of you were wonderful when you played doubles together before."

"I still don't know," my dad says, shaking his head. "As we've been telling you, playing at that level requires a certain type of commitment. That's a commitment you weren't prepared for previously, Maggie."

"I'm committed to BMX."

"I'm sure, sweetie," Mom says in a tone so patronizing it makes my skin crawl.

"Maybe you can try out for the volleyball team?" my dad adds. "That way you can start over without ruining things for your sister."

"Ruining things for my sister!" I exclaim. "I knew it! Is that really what you think I'd do?"

"Well, your history—"

"Screw my history. Just admit that this is 100 percent about Bella, isn't it? Why are you are always so worried about her? Why don't you ever worry about me?"

"That's not true, Maggie. We just think that—"

"I'd be doing her a favor anyway."

"A favor?" Bella sits up straighter. "You think I need you?"

"You need me if you want to win more matches," I mutter.

"How can you say that?" Her face pales.

"Maggie, leave your sister out of it. This is about you."

"Is it? Well, then, I've made up my mind. Count me in," I slam my empty cup on the table. "But I'm not wearing that stupid skort."

I storm out of the restaurant and jump on my bike to pedal to the skate park. It's not until later that I realize what I just got myself into.

Chapter 4
BELLA

I've always loved the first day of school. Everything is new: new notebooks, new clothes, new bags, and new beginnings. And this year, a brand-new campus for us since B-Dub High is about a mile down the road from the middle school.

If I take away the whole Maggie infringing on my tennis dreams thing (which I'm beginning to have second thoughts about—the big reveal to our parents didn't exactly go as I'd hoped) and the fact that we're in the same creative writing class (I mean, can I ever escape her?), my day has lived up to the anticipatory hype.

With my pink Prince bag smacking against my back, I rush with Sadie, who played with me on the middle school tennis team, toward the Beachwood Sports Compound immediately after school. The brand-new outdoor tennis facility sits beyond the football and track stadium, and even though Maggie and I live only a bike ride away from Beachwood Academy, I haven't had a chance to peek at it. I was too busy training with Joe and traveling to tournaments to make it to school during the break.

The breath whooshes from my lungs as we walk together through the vast entranceway. I feel the butterflies flapping in my stomach as I stare out at the four royal blue courts lined up side by side like rectangular squares on a Hershey bar. About thirty girls scurry around. I glance at them, taking note of who's practicing with whom and who's wearing what, and gulp when I catch sight of Lauren and Minka warming up in the far corner. The butterflies flap even more ferociously. Even though Coach Kasinski practically recruited me and my sister, I'm still a little nervous about making varsity. Obviously, I don't want to end up on some stupid freshman team.

"Wow," Sadie gasps as she takes in the tremendous compound.

"Thought you came to get an early look at this place over the summer."

"I did, but it doesn't get old," Sadie says, shrugging.

"That must be Coach's office?" I say, pointing to a free-standing building with a large window that overlooks the hard courts.

"Yeah, I think so," Sadie answers as she pulls out a Head racquet like mine. Her tiny gemstone nose stud shimmers in the sun. "Looks like the locker rooms are next door."

We pass a group of local sports reporters clutching notebooks and waiting eagerly outside the office for a pre-season interview with Coach Kasinski. My nerve endings tingle with all the excitement in the air—it's crazy to me that all these people are here to see the woman who will hopefully guide my high school tennis career and catapult me into the upper rankings . . . albeit with my sister by my side.

As soon as Coach Kasinski opens the door, the reporters begin peppering her with questions. "Coach, are you ready for the new season?" a reporter with a pencil tucked behind his ear asks.

"Of course." Coach beams as Martie, Beachwood's athletic director, walks out from the locker rooms onto the complex and surveys the scene before hurrying over to join Coach Kasinski.

"How do you do it, Coach?" a man wearing a red collegiate cap asks. "How do you manage to coach so many championships when you couldn't win one as a pro?"

Coach's forehead wrinkles. She begins to open her mouth, her face turning scarlet, when Martie intervenes and escorts the reporter away.

"Yikes," I say when the reporters have dispersed. "Did you hear that guy?"

"Yeah," Sadie replies, shaking her head. "That's messed up."

"I thought Coach Kasinski was pretty amazing when she played."

"She was, but the guy's right. She was ranked pretty high but never won anything until she became a coach. All the older girls were gossiping about it when I came to look at the complex a few weeks back."

"That's kind of a weird thing for them to be talking about, isn't it?" I cock my head to the side.

"Yeah, I think they were just annoyed at Coach or something."

"Really? Why?" I stop mid-stride, crossing my arms.

"No idea. All I know is that apparently there was a lot of hype and some people felt like she never lived up to it."

"That stinks. I guess she made up for it as a coach." I shrug.

"Anyway, enough speculating about Coach Kasinski's history. Wanna warm up?"

"Do you even have to ask?"

"Nah, stupid question I guess." Sadie and I always warm up together since she's also coached by Joe. "Want to go over there?" I point to the court next to where Minka and Lauren are warming up. I'm desperate to study their technique despite what Coach says about their not being as good as they once were.

Sadie looks over at Lauren and Minka and grins. "Sure!" Then she whispers, "This is so cool! I can't believe we're going to warm up so close to the two of them."

I nod enthusiastically, returning her wide smile with an even bigger one of my own. "I know!" I whisper-scream in response.

"You at least get to see them at tournaments. I barely ever do."

"Yeah, sometimes, but not that much. We're still in different age brackets." I unzip my bag and pull out my lucky purple racquet. "Besides you're busy doing other stuff." While I'm super-serious about tennis, Sadie splits her time between the courts and the Venice art scene. Most of the time she prefers painting canvases to dominating courts.

"Yeah, but still . . ." Sadie presses, leaning into me.

"Okay, okay!" I beam, overwhelmed with the feeling that this is going to be the best tennis season ever. As I bend down to grab a tennis ball from a wire bucket, I spot my sister. I squeeze my eyes shut in a silent prayer—*please, oh please, let her be serious about this.* Opening them, I discover that, of course, she's clad in Vans and a black Sector cap pulled low over her poker-straight locks. White earbuds are stuck in her ears, and her old Wilson racquet leans against her leg as she haphazardly stretches in the corner.

"Oh my God." Sadie nudges me from behind, causing me to jump. "Is that your sister? What is Maggie doing here?"

I just shrug, hoping Sadie will drop the Maggie subject before I have to explain Coach's whole plan to her.

"Isn't she into, like, BMX or something?" Sadie continues to prod. "I see her at the Venice skate park all the time."

I shrug again. "Yeah, I guess." I pick up a fuzzy tennis ball and balance it on the strings of my racquet, hoping beyond hope that Maggie doesn't make a fool of me. "She's kind of been into a lot of stuff." I let the ball drop and begin to tap it, forcing myself to concentrate on my game. "So remember what Joe said before he left for the Open—Coach loves to see perfect form. She's tough on technique."

Sadie nods in agreement. "Yep!"

We take a few steps away from each other and begin to hit lightly back and forth over the net, falling into our usual rhythm.

From out of the corner of my eye, I glance at Lauren and Minka. The dynamic duo is dressed in matching tennis attire—powder-blue-and-white lined skorts with Dri-FIT white tanks. Their long blonde ponytails sway with each perfect stroke. Minka, a junior, always gives the best answers in interviews while Lauren, a senior, looks like she could grace the covers of magazines. I would kill to get the kind of attention they do.

"God, that racquet is really working!" Minka says to her older sister. A large rhinestone-encrusted L sparkles on the side of Lauren's brand-new Prince racquet.

"I told you. You should have picked one up too." Lauren hits the ball back to her sister. "Instead of that Tory Burch bracelet you bought yesterday."

I can't believe I'm good enough to be sharing the court with Lauren and Minka. And I still can't believe that Coach Kasinski said they've plateaued after they placed so high on the Junior circuit last year. When I squat into my ready position and look down at my racquet, it's shaking.

"I've got plenty of new lucky clothes and a lucky bag. And don't forget our new lucky court?" Minka says.

"It's to die," Lauren says, hitting a crosscourt shot.

"Totally fantabulous."

They burst into a giggle fit.

"Earth to Bella!" Sadie calls when she catches me staring.

Minka and Lauren glance our way when they hear Sadie, then shrug at each other, never breaking their rhythm.

My cheeks burn—and not from the warm sun—as Sadie serves the ball my way. This is it! I'm actually standing here, practicing on the Beachwood Academy tennis courts. All my nervous anticipation of tryouts, all the dreams and excitement I've bottled up since I started playing tennis explode into my backhand.

"Girl, you got it going *on* today. Nice shot," Sadie says as my passing shot flies by her. She turns around to grab another ball.

"Thanks," I say. A flush runs up my back. I hope that Coach Kasinski will feel the same way.

While Sadie and I practice our fore- and backhands, we cover everything from our first day of school to cute guys to tennis. But it's hard to be totally excited by our conversation because I can't help but look behind me to check on Maggie every five seconds. Instead of practicing like everyone else, she continues to stretch, bobbing her head to either Lil Wayne or worse, Public Enemy.

"Are we done yet?" Lauren yells out, surprising me. I would have expected her to be as pumped about the first day of the new season as I am.

"So soon?" Minka shouts.

"We've been playing for, like, twenty minutes, and I already trained this morning," Lauren whines, bending over to touch her toes. She waves animatedly to a surfer-looking guy in the stands.

He tilts his head and gives her a little nod, a glossy look in his eyes.

"Fine." Minka catches her sister's volley. She shoves two tennis balls into the side pocket of her skort, while Lauren adjusts her long flaxen pony.

"You have a twin?" Minka calls, as I'm about to toss the ball into the air for a serve.

I freeze, squeezing the ball in my left hand. "You mean me?"

"Well, duh, who else is there?" Lauren says, adjusting her tank. "Minka and I were just saying that you and that girl over there—who's your twin, right?—look like brunette versions of Maria Sharapova."

I look over at Maggie still rocking out to her iPod. "Yeah, that's my sister."

"You're genetically identical," Sadie whispers, having just walked over. "It's kinda obvious."

"Shh . . ." I whisper back.

Sadie shakes her head. "Since you're busy with these two

geniuses, I'm gonna go pick up the balls we left on the court, okay?" she asks.

I nod in response.

"Hey, that must be the girl who was riding her bike outside the hotel during the Memorial Day tournament in Colorado!" Minka looks up at her sister.

"I think it might be," Lauren replies. "I remember her having no fashion sense."

The two of them snicker, then skip over to our court. "Yeah. That's definitely her," Minka announces, squinting her heavily mascaraed eyes at Maggie.

"You know," Lauren says, turning to face me. Now that she's standing next to me, I realize that she's not just slightly taller than I am, but that she towers over me. There must be a difference of at least five inches. "We almost lost our match the next morning because I was so tired from the banging sound of her bike."

"Yeah, we thought it was you at first, but couldn't figure out why you'd go all, like, grunge or whatever," Minka adds in her raspy voice. She's probably three inches shorter than her sister, and up close I can see that she has more freckles than Lindsay Lohan.

"Oh. Sorry about that." I try to count the freckles on Minka's ear as my face heats up. "Maggie is really into bikes."

Lauren and Minka smirk at each other like they're in on a joke I'm not privy to. For a second, I yearn for the type of sister relationship they share. They both like the same things. They have each other's backs. They don't embarrass each other.

"Well, at least they're not playing doubles, like us," Minka says to Lauren almost like I'm not even there.

"I know. Can you imagine?" Laurens responds, placing her French manicured fingers in front of her full lips. "Like, what a disaster. That girl is a mess."

I wipe my sweaty palms on the side of my Adidas tennis dress.

Lauren looks over at Maggie, then Minka leans in, whispering something to her sister. They both giggle as Maggie walks toward me.

This isn't good. Maggie is known to blow her temper, especially around "clones," which is what she calls Minka and Lauren and pretty much everyone else who plays tennis.

I intercept my sister before she picks up on Lauren and Minka's attitude. The last thing I need is for Maggie to get into fisticuffs with my potential teammates.

The O'Donnell girls continue to snicker behind us.

"Hey, sista!" Maggie says with sarcastic enthusiasm. She bends over to stretch and quickly touches her Vans. "Ready to play some tennis?" She poses with her racquet.

Sadie makes her way over to us after having finished up her ball-hopper duties.

I stare at my sister and shake my head.

"What?" she asks, shrugging.

What is Maggie *really* doing here? Sure, she's a natural athlete, but why'd she suddenly decide to try out with me? She gave up on tennis a long time ago, so why now? Why tennis?

I open my mouth to ask her that very question when a woman

who I assume is an assistant coach interrupts us. "Okay, ladies, gather round please!" she shouts.

"Lauren and Minka!" Coach Kasinski yells. "A *Daily News* reporter wants to interview you." She turns to the woman who called us together and says, "I'm going to head over with them. I'll be right back. You get the girls started without me."

Lauren and Minka show off their pearly whites and jog to join the reporter, Lauren waving to the surfer guy as she goes.

I don't remember Lauren ever dating anyone before. . . .

I glance at Maggie, who is shaking out her arms. Then, I stare at the reporters. I'm guessing that Minka and Lauren are getting interviewed because they pulled off that upset at the Juniors. Now they're like rock stars. I'd give anything to be the person the reporters want to talk to.

I look over at Maggie and take a deep breath. Is Coach Kasinski right? Could Maggie really be my ticket to that kind of glory? Could Maggie and I really get a shot at the California Classic and maybe even a boost in the rankings?

"Hello everyone, I'm one of Coach Kasinski's assistants," the woman standing alongside us says, confirming my suspicions. "We're going to begin tryouts today by looking at your overall game. Does anyone have any general questions before we commence?"

No one says anything, not even Maggie, who usually relishes the chance to throw a silly question at any kind of authority figure.

"Great. Let's get started," the assistant says.

I follow everyone to the edge of the baseline.

"We'll split you into two groups. One group will stay with Coach

Kasinski and me. The other will go to the adjacent court"—the assistant nods to the far court—"to be evaluated by two of our other assistant coaches."

Minka and Lauren return from their interviews and cut in line behind Maggie and me. No one says a word about how they should go to the back of the line. Except for Maggie, of course.

"Hey," she says. "What are you—"

I nudge her.

Lauren and Minka are obviously the queens of this court and as far as I'm concerned, they've earned it.

We're split in half, and Maggie, Sadie, Lauren, Minka, and another ten or so girls I don't recognize line up behind me. The rest of the girls join the two assistants on the other court.

Coach Kasinski ambles over, smiling and throwing one last friendly wave to the reporters. "My favorite part. Tryouts!" Coach Kasinski shouts, clapping her hands. "I love to see who really has it in them to take this franchise—and their game—to the next level."

Sadie and I nervously look at each other.

"I'm looking for girls who play the Kasinski way. If I don't think you're my kind of player, then"—she runs her finger along her neck in a slicing motion—"you're out. Gone. I don't have time for losers."

I take a deep breath. *This is it! My chance to shine!*

Right on cue, Coach calls out, "Bella Anderson, you're up first."

Within seconds, I'm rocking back and forth on the soles of my feet behind the baseline. I focus on my breathing.

"Ready?" Coach calls.

I nod.

She tosses me a ball.

I catch it. I can feel Coach's eyes and the eyes of the rest of the girls in line on me. The assistant coach stands on the other side of the net, ready to return my serve.

I toss the ball into the air.

My stomach tightens as an image of me double faulting and losing the final game at the Memorial Day tournament flashes in front of my eyes.

I can't do it. What if Coach Kasinski sees right through me? What if she doesn't think I have what it takes to play the Kasinski way? What if it's really Maggie she's after? I catch the ball.

I have to do it. I think of the quote Joe always offers: "Pressure is a privilege."

I toss the ball into the air again. This time I swing my racquet over my head.

Thwack.

The ball lands deep in the service box.

Yes!

The assistant returns the serve. I loosen my grip on the racquet, then squeeze as the ball hits the sweet spot. I whack the ball with a perfect two-handed backhand.

Thwack.

The assistant returns another shot with a forehand.

"Low to high," Coach Kasinski yells.

I'm not sure whether I should be offended—that instruction is pretty elementary. Still, I make sure to exaggerate my low to high forehand with the next hit.

"That's it!" Coach Kasinski shouts.

I feel my heart burst with excitement. I've already managed to please her.

The assistant drop-shots the ball, barely over the net this time.

"Run the ball down!" Coach yells to me. "One hand it if you have to."

I barely manage a nod before I slide across the court with no thought to the consequences and poke the ball. As I do, I realize that I must have just scraped my shin on the hard surface.

"Yes!" Coach Kasinski cheers. "Now see your opening!"

The assistant coach charges the net and hits another drop shot back to me. I don't have time to check the graze on my shin. I stand up and sprint to the ball. I spot my opening.

Thwack.

I volley the ball past my opponent. It hits just inside the baseline behind her.

Coach Kasinski claps loudly and whistles. "Well played! Beautiful finesse, Bella. I caught a glimpse of myself as a young player there."

Coach's high praise and my knockout performance bring a happy glow to my cheeks. I couldn't have done it without her calling the shots. She really is a great coach. A smile spreads across my face as I think how I just managed to win a point off the assistant coach.

I jog to the end of the line and am met with varied reactions from the other players. Sadie gives me a high five. Lauren and Minka stare at me blankly. And Maggie mouths, "Nice job," and then, "your leg." I look down at my shin. It's seen better days, but I try not to focus on the damage.

Scrape or not, I'm golden.

"Okay, Maggie Anderson, the hidden jewel I discovered yesterday, you're up!" Coach Kasinski glances at her clipboard. "I've been looking forward to this all day."

I cringe. Here we go. I hope she doesn't embarrass herself too badly.

Sadie looks over her shoulder at me. She juts out her lip in sympathy, obviously sensing how worried I am about this whole thing. Lauren and Minka whisper to each other loudly. Then Lauren loses interest in the conversation and appears distracted. I wonder if she's thinking about her new boy toy.

Maggie steps behind the baseline. She bounces the ball twice on the back of her hand then once on the ground.

"Okay. Enough silly games, John McEnroe. Let's go," Coach Kasinski says.

I cringe. This is typical Maggie. She used to always say that she needed to do her "lucky bounces" before serving.

Sure enough, my sister shouts, "It's for good luck!"

Sadie turns around and bugs her eyes at me as if to say, *Can you believe she just said that?*

Coach Kasinski scribbles across her clipboard as Maggie tosses the ball into the air.

Thwack.

She manages to hit the ball into the service box. Her serve is certainly not anywhere near as refined as mine or technically sound, but it's wide and powerful enough to hit just inside the doubles alley with force.

The assistant returns the serve to Maggie's forehand.

Thwack.

Maggie shuffles and shows off her powerful swing.

"Remember low to high," Coach Kasinski instructs, same as she did with me.

The ball ricochets off the court and takes a tough spin, but the assistant gets to it and sends another ball to Maggie's forehand. Ignoring Coach Kasinski's instructions, Maggie hits the ball exactly the same way.

"Low to high!" Coach shouts louder this time, smacking her clipboard.

Maggie's always been this way on the court. Her playing style is more intuitive than conscious.

The assistant must take Maggie's failure to follow Coach's instructions as a sign that she doesn't have what it takes because, sure enough, she soon underestimates her ability. She can't catch up to the ball, misjudges the spin, and misses her shot. The ball smacks the net.

Minka and Lauren gasp in unison.

Maggie turns around and smiles at Coach Kasinski. "You like?" she says.

Oh my God.

Coach glares at Maggie. She tucks her clipboard under her well-defined arm. "You are very lucky you are so talented, young lady, or this would be over for you right now. If you want to play on this court, do not ever ignore my instructions again. And if you want to work with a coach of my stature, you will remember you are lucky to share this complex with me and the other girls who I select for our elite team. Do I make myself clear?"

I stare at my tennis shoes, embarrassed. Why does Maggie have to be so disrespectful?

"Yes, *Coach K*. I understand perfectly. Thank you," Maggie says, her sloppy Vans slapping against the composite as she scurries over to me.

Did my sister seriously just call the venerable Olga Kasinski by a patronizing nickname?

"Coach K?" Kasinski repeats. "I don't remember telling you that you could call me that."

I brace myself, expecting Maggie to say something rude in response, but she just shrugs.

"If you need a lesson on appropriate behavior—like how to keep your mouth shut, accept authority, and listen to instruction—you might want to pay attention to your sister," Coach spews at Maggie. "And the next time you're lucky enough to set foot on my court, show some respect and dress properly."

"Yes, ma'am."

I close my eyes, willing it all to be over. When I finally have the courage to look, I see Maggie is behind me smirking. "Did you see that shot?" she asks. "I think I made the team."

"Shhh!" I say as Coach continues to glower. She looks down at her clipboard and shakes her head, muttering, "Talent is such a curse."

Chapter Five
MAGGIE

The skate park in Venice Beach is surprisingly uncrowded for a Friday night.

After staring at the sun sinking into the Pacific for a few minutes, I listen to the click and clunk of skateboarders riding the gray steps as I breathe in the salty air. I buckle the helmet straps under my chin.

God I love this park. In fact, I think it's the only thing that got me through the first full week of school: knowing that I'd see the usual group of guys and girls for a bike sesh. Unlike my boyfriend, Ryan, most of the other BMXers don't attend B-Dub, so the only time I get to see the crew is at the park.

"Nice lid," Ryan says, smacking the top of my blue helmet. He lets his hand fall to my back for a moment. His simple touch sends a wave of shivers down my spine. I look up at him and am blown away—not for the first time—by how totally gorgeous and awesome he is.

"When are you going to start wearing one?" I ask, mounting my blue Mongoose and squeezing the black grips on the handlebars as Ryan and I roll up to the gray concrete table separating two quarter pipes. The park has so many varied elements—everything from street-style obstacles like stairs with railings to boxes, ledges, and a variety of bowls and ramps—it's a blast to ride here.

Ryan immediately drops in and his tires rub against the concrete as he gains momentum on the vert. "It's all good, Mags." He continues up and down the sides of the ramp, gaining momentum, his big smile infectious.

I shake my head and remind myself not to act like Bella and my parents. I want him to be safe, but I'm not his boss. It's his noggin. And one of the things that I love most about Ryan is how laid back he is.

I watch Ryan pedal, reaching for my phone when I feel it buzz in the back pocket of my jeans. It's Bella asking what park I'm at tonight, which is weird since she usually doesn't care. I text her back and remind her that it's Friday and she should actually be out having fun. I doubt she'll heed my advice. I'm sure she's at Beachwood hitting tennis balls. Speaking of, I wonder when Coach K—that's what I'm calling her from now on since it's way less of a mouthful—will post the roster. I'm kind of dying to know if I pulled it off and made the team. Can't wait to see how my parents react to that one. They'll probably use the laces from my old tennis shoes to tie me to my bed frame for fear that I'll get out of the house and ruin things for their *perfect* daughter.

Below me in the pipe, Ryan's standing on his pedals and gaining intense speed. "Watch this can-can," Ryan yells to his friend, a guy with a buzz cut who's standing next to me waiting his turn.

"You're sick, dude," a guy covered in tattoos shouts, straddling his bike.

Once Ryan reaches the coping, he's airborne. He lifts his left leg off the pedal and moves it over the bike tube. Then, he dramatically leans his body one way while moving his bike the other, completing a 180. In an instant, he moves his feet back on the pedals and he's back on the seat.

Thump.

Both tires hit the ramp at the same time and Ryan rolls down the transition triumphantly.

I whistle and cheer. Every time Ryan nails a trick, it makes me want to get out there and nail it myself.

"Wow. Man! You blasted that!" a girl with long blonde hair tucked under a camouflage hat yells as we all watch in amazement. "X Games are within reach." She jostles back and forth on her pink Mongoose bike.

"That's what I'm hoping," Ryan calls. His eyes and smile are wider than the pipe, like they always are when he lands a trick. "And I'll be bringing Maggie with me."

"Well, I don't think I'll be competing," I say. Big competitions are not really my thing, not after my last one ended in my breaking someone's nose.

"Aw. You'll be cheering for your boy in the stands," the guy with the buzz cut taunts. "How cute."

"I'm not saying I *couldn't*—I'm saying I do this for fun." I push on my pegs with my feet to make sure they're tight. "Competition's not for me. It turns people psychotic." It occurs to me that there's a chance I could end up eating my own words when it comes to tennis, but I refuse to let myself think about that.

"Yeah, and I'm sure you're declining comp-invites with your killer 180s." The tattooed guy smirks.

"Hey, you gotta cut me some slack. I just started them two weeks ago." I take a moment to enjoy the view from my perch atop the table. It may be dark but I can still make out the sand and sea stretching out for miles.

Ryan stops in front of me, smiles, and pecks me on the lips. He tastes sweet from the Now and Laters he chews when he rides and I can detect the smell of salt on him, a combination of hard-earned sweat and ocean air. "That one was for you, Mags."

Well, that's definitely something tennis is missing besides the sense of adventure—kisses from my boyfriend.

"Who's up next?" another girl yells, antsy for her turn.

"Me." I look down into the steep bowl.

I take a breath to prepare for dropping in. I push off the coping, lean to the side, and drop into the bowl. I sail down and as I'm ascending the other side, I pump the transition with my sore legs (thanks, tennis) for more speed.

Once I feel like I'm fast enough, I push the pedals even harder. I reach the top of the jump but turn my handlebars right so that I reverse and ride back down the side of the bowl, enjoying the rush even though I don't actually do any extreme jumping or anything.

"Aw. Come on," one of Ryan's friends yells, straddling his bike next to Ryan on the table watching me.

"You can do it!" Ryan yells.

Adrenaline pumping through my blood, I ride faster this time up the side, and before I hit the coping, I gain air. This time, I don't look down and complete the 180.

Thump.

Hell's yeah! I ride up the vert and brake on the flat.

"Sick," Ryan yells, touching my arm as I ride by. With my blood pumping from the rush, I continue up the side and climb onto the concrete table. Then I roll by the crew and down the ramp. Instead of staying in the pipe, I head toward the skateboarders.

I skateboarded for a bit before I got bored with it. That's when Ryan found me: watching the freestyle riders instead of practicing my ollies. Once I discovered BMX, I dumped my board for a bike, but I still rip a bit on the longboard for fun.

I take on a short ramp adjacent to the pipe, jump slightly with both tires off the ground, and complete a simple bunny hop.

Ryan rides up next to me. He wraps his arm around me and squeezes. I lean my head against his shoulder, still sitting on my bike. There is nowhere else I'd rather be right now. There's nothing better than the hum of tires on the ramp mixed with the sounds of the Venice Beach Boardwalk—the zooming of roller-bladers, the excited squawking of the seagulls, the drum circle at the front of the park. The smell of Big Daddy's Pizza tickles my nose.

"So, I have something to tell you . . ." I say to Ryan.

"Yeah?" Ryan pulls off his black knit hat, showing his crystal-blue eyes.

"I tried out for the tennis team."

"Is that where you were after school? I thought you checked out on me." Ryan squeezes me tighter, then runs his other hand through his curly blond locks.

"Are you crazy?" I trace my index finger over his cheek. "I would never check out on you."

"I didn't even know you played tennis." He shifts on his bike.

"I know," I say. "I don't really. I mean, I haven't since I was basically a kid. The coach invited me to try out while I was practicing with Bella last weekend. I figured I'd give it another shot."

In the background I can hear our friends yelling in excitement. Someone must have nailed a cool trick.

"I can't say I'm surprised you got recruited. You picked up BMX pretty fast. You're one heck of an athlete."

I look down at my black Vans. My face burns.

"So why did you stop playing in the first place?"

"Long story. But don't worry. I've got it under control now."

"How so?" Ryan asks, pulling up his jeans, which sag when he rides.

I'm always surprised when it comes to Ryan. Other guys I've hung out with talked a lot but never really asked about me. I think they just liked me because I could keep up with them.

I roll my bike's fat tires forward, then backward. "The whole tennis thing is just part of my master plan."

"What do you mean?" Ryan asks.

Before I can answer, one of our friends pulls up on her Haro bike, balancing on the table. She gives me a wounded look. "Did you say tennis, Mags? Really?"

I shrug. "Just tired of Bella getting all the fame and glory, you know?"

"I've got a sister like that at home," she says, adjusting her gloves. "Like cheerleading is some great achievement."

"Well," I say, "tennis is at least a legit sport."

"Have you seen the girls that play? They're the biggest snobs." She scrunches her nose like there's an odor in the air, then rides off to get some air on the pipe.

"You know, I think Maggie's got some major cojones to go out on the court and mix it up with B-Dub's finest!" Ryan calls after her.

"Hey, who knows?" I say to Ryan, turning my bike so that I'm facing him directly. "Maybe if my family sees me rack up some tennis trophies, they'll take the riding more seriously."

"Is that what this is about?" Ryan asks, placing his knit hat back on his head.

"Sort of."

"You know, no one gives this sport the respect it deserves. Most people think we just hang out here and ride our bikes like we're six."

"Yeah, that's part of it, but it's more than that."

Ryan obviously misunderstands my meaning because he says, "Really, Mags, you don't need to feel like it's your job to force people to get BMX." He gives me a quick peck. "My mom sometimes says I should ride my beach cruiser to the park. Get some use out of it."

I giggle at that one, letting my frustrations with my parents fall into the backdrop. "Can you imagine hucking tricks on a cruiser? I'd like to see that."

"I know, right?" Ryan cracks up, shaking his head. "Ready for this?"

"Which one?"

"Maybe a dipped 360."

"That move is crazy!"

"Watch me!" Ryan drops in and coasts down the vert. Once he reaches the top of the pipe, he airs out, almost getting high enough to be eye level with me on the table.

I swallow hard as I watch him in the darkening sky. The other guys I've hung out with were fearless, but Ryan takes it to a whole other level. At the last second, he hangs up on the coping. He face twists.

I hide my eyes so I don't see him wipe out.

"Oh, man!" someone screams.

But, instead of a thump, I hear a swish.

When I turn back around, Ryan is knee-skating down the bowl with his hands out, showboating. His bike slides behind him.

"You almost bit it!" a guy yells, shaking his head. "Good thing you're wearing jeans."

"I'm like a cat." Ryan shouts, grinning.

"A cat?" I drop my bike and ride down the pipe to Ryan's side. I jump off my bike and pull him in for a hug.

"I always land on my feet," he says, grinning. His jeans are ripped at the knees. "Or you know, somewhere cool."

"Oh, I thought you were gonna say that you've got nine lives."

Ryan's grin grows even wider. "That too."

I let go of Ryan when I hear the flap of approaching flip-flops and look up to see my sister nervously making her way over and around the obstacles. She teeters on a ledge, looking down at me in the bowl. At the same time, she is almost taken out by a skateboarder.

"Mags!" Bella screeches. A white and royal blue leather bag is slung over her left shoulder. "There you are." She places her hands against her hips where her white sweater grazes the top of her skinny jeans.

"Hey, Bella," Ryan calls, nodding at her before he hops on his bike and begins to ride up the vert again, no hesitation.

"Hi Ryan." She responds in the same dismissive tone my mother uses with me. He's gone before he can hear her. Bella's eyes move from side to side as she nervously surveys the site. Another skate-boarder rolls by, causing her to jump. She slowly climbs down a ramp to the mini and ledges.

"What's up, Bella? Come to have some fun tonight?" I ask. "That's so unlike you."

"Fat chance." She rolls her blue eyes. "Grace and I were on our way to pick up Sadie, so I figured I'd stop by the park."

"That was awfully kind of you," I say. "But don't you usually spend Friday nights hitting balls?"

"Ha ha." She steps aside to let a skateboarder roll by. The dude mumbles something about poseurs as he passes us. "Whatever. I'm doing you a favor."

"Lucky me." I stop in front of a low rail.

Bella daintily steps over it.

"You missed tonight's meeting." Bella's pink lip gloss glistens. "Coach was not happy."

"Oops." I look up to see Ryan on the table. "I guess I lost track of time. Coach K must have really missed me."

Bella drops the bag she's carrying on the ground, then looks at the stained concrete and thinks twice. She picks the bag up, dusting it off with the edge of her sweater. "Can you be serious for one second?"

"All right. All right," I say, laughing. "What did I miss?"

She hops a bit and claps like a cheerleader. "I made the team!"

"Of course you did," I say, looking up at my friends again. They're on the ledge.

"And so did you," she says, less excitement in her voice this time. She hands over the leather bag. "We're the number two doubles team, behind Minka and Lauren. And they're the team co-captains, of course."

"What about singles?" I try not to sound nervous.

"Yes, I am number seven out of eight, barely varsity for now." Bella lets out a sigh.

I give her a go-on look.

"Oh, you didn't make the singles team," she says, almost sounding relieved.

I nearly breathe my own sigh—whether also of relief or of disappointment, I'm not totally sure. But I stop myself. I don't want the BMX crew to witness that kind of display of emotion. I'm in control here.

"Anyway, your uniform is in the bag along with a black skort, socks, a visor, and a Beachwood tennis tank. Check it out; it's pretty." She looks over at Ryan, who's stopped biking and is headed our way.

"I'm not wearing—"

"Look, Maggie, you made it this far. All I ask is that whatever you're doing, don't screw this up for me."

"I'm not—"

"At this point, I really don't care. Just, like I said, if you're going to go through with this, please don't mess up what I've worked so hard to achieve."

Before I can open my mouth, Bella waves hastily at me and turns around. "See you at home," she says. She scurries daintily up the wall and walks quickly across the skate park. Two of our friends stop and whistle at her, probably to tease me more than anything.

I stare at the stiff leather bag, my nose crinkled in disdain.

Ryan is at my side now and drapes his arm across my shoulders.

"What have we here?" Ryan's friend with the buzz cut asks, rolling up and snatching the bag from my grasp. "Ooh, nice skirt!" He snickers, holding it up and wiggling it around.

It's a skort, though I'd never tell him that. "Just give it here," I say, holding out my hand.

"Almost as good as a cheerleader outfit!" He holds it against himself as if trying it on, looking utterly ridiculous the whole time.

I grab it back from him and stuff it into the leather bag, though I don't know who I'm fooling. I'm sure it'll look just as silly on me.

Chapter Six
BELLA

"I can't believe Maggie made the team," Sadie whispers to me as we move our desks together during third period creative writing on Monday.

I can't tell if she's upset or not—she only nailed the alternate singles spot on junior varsity, so it must be weird for her that Maggie, who hasn't played in years, made it to doubles varsity.

"Shhh!" Mr. Ludwig says, making an ugly face in the front of the room. "Remember this is a group project. No clowning around. You have plenty of questions to keep you busy." He plops down in his desk chair and focuses on a giant stack of papers in front of him.

I hang my head as I straighten my desk and take out my pink binder. I set it neatly in the middle of my desk and lay two freshly sharpened pencils next to it.

"Wait. What? What's going on?" Grace, looking dumbfounded, joins us. She drops two chunky picture books and a packet of questions on the desk. I'm so glad I get to take a class with Grace. She's older than me, but creative writing is an elective, so we were both able to register.

Why Maggie also registered is anyone's guess.

"We have to analyze the picture books," I say, picking up my pencil and hoping to switch the subject from my sister back to the task at hand. I begin to read the first question out loud.

"No, no, not that." Grace shakes her head. Her braid swings like a horse's tail. "I'm talking about Maggie," she says, glancing over at her and Ryan. "She's on the tennis team?"

"Yeah, it's no big." I shake her off.

"No big? Maggie hasn't played in forever! And now she's your doubles partner," Sadie says.

"Really. It's nothing," I say as nonchalantly as I can manage.

Grace looks at me in wide-eyed disbelief. Instead of saying more, I cast my eyes down and begin our assignment. Sadie takes the opportunity to catch Grace up on Maggie's surprising new foray into tennis. I glance up from the questions and sneak a peek at my sister across the classroom. She and her latest boyfriend are nestled close to each other in the corner, comfortably flipping through a BMX Plus! magazine. Their question sheets and picture books are nowhere in sight.

For a second, I feel a tiny stab of jealousy over Maggie and Ryan's six-month relationship. Maggie almost always has a boyfriend, and even when they break up, they usually stay friends. I'm too busy for that.

Before I feel sorry for myself, I remember what Joe always says. I'll have plenty of time for boys *after* tennis. He's right.

"Holy tutus," Grace screeches, picking up her purple pen and pulling me out of my reverie. "How do you feel about all this, Bells?"

I shrug and yawn. After an exhibition match in Torrance yesterday, I'm wiped.

"Can you imagine?" Sadie's blue eyes bug. She tucks a piece of ebony hair behind her ear. "Finally, you have your shot playing varsity for B-Dub and here comes your sister, ready to screw it up for you."

"Poor Bella." Grace shakes her head.

"So frustrating, right? Bella is an amazing finesse player, but Maggie has that lefty advantage and she covers the court amazingly. How totally unfair," Sadie adds.

"Gee thanks," I say, looking up from the picture book.

"That totally came out wrong. You know what I mean," Sadie says, pulling a chunk of hair in front of her face and searching for split ends.

"Like if you put Maggie and Bella together, they make the perfect player?" Grace asks.

"Exactly." Sadie adjusts her cardigan over the short silky dress cinched at her waist with a patent leather belt. "But how annoying for Bella."

Maggie looks over her shoulder at us. I can tell she knows we're talking about her, and I don't want her to overhear. She'll get annoyed and I'll have to deal with it later.

"And Maggie's such a natural," Sadie adds, loudly. "Too bad she has zero commitment. She'd probably be ranked internationally if she showed the dedication Bella does to tennis."

Ouch.

"Shh," I say for more than one reason.

Sadie ignores me. She leans over the latest copy of *Tennishead* magazine. Her dark hair skims the pages.

"No fun for Bella." Grace sticks out her glossed bottom lip in sympathy.

"Really. I'm cool with it," I lie and search my bag for a can of Diet Coke. Something to wake me up. "We really need to get going on this."

"You're a better person than me, Bella," Sadie says. "I'd hang myself if I were you right now." She twists her nose piercing.

I crack open my can. Ludwig looks up at the loud fizzing.

"And check out Maggie over there, reading some skating magazine with Ryan and totally blowing off the assignment," Grace says.

"You mean like we're doing?" I tease. I don't bother correcting Grace on the difference between BMX and skating.

"I don't think she really cares about tennis," Grace says, pushing her long locks over her shoulders.

"Who told you?" Sadie replies, deadpan.

"Do you think it's a sibling rivalry thing?" Grace asks us.

"Could be." Sadie's eyes widen. "Remember when Lauren hooked up with Minka's boyfriend?"

"Wait. What?" I say, looking up from the binder.

"Yup. That was before Lauren started dating Brandon Teisch like a month ago. Anyway, I heard that last year Lauren said she kissed this guy to prove to Minka that he was a jerk. And get this: Minka actually thanked her for it."

Okay, scratch what I thought at tryouts. Maybe I don't want a bond *exactly* like theirs.

Sadie, already bored with the gossip, points at a photo of Rafael Nadal in her magazine. "Look, there's my boyfriend."

I peek at the picture of my favorite tennis hottie. "I'll sacrifice myself to prove to you that he's not good enough for you," I say dramatically.

We break out in giggles, and Maggie looks over her shoulder at us again.

"Can you imagine kissing him?" Sadie says. "Yum-my!"

"Let me see that magazine," I say, reaching for Sadie's copy of *Tennishead*. Out of the corner of my eye, I see Maggie continue to flip through her bike magazine, assured that we're not talking about her.

"Oh, check this out," I say, pointing at an ad for an orange and gray Nike tennis dress in the magazine. "You like?"

"Let me see." Grace leans over her desk. "I think the blue one would look amazing on you, Bella. It would show off your eyes. And maybe purple for Sadie since her hair is so dark and her eyes are so light. Only certain people can pull off purple and make it work."

"We really need to review our answers to Ludwig's questions and finish analyzing these books," I say, shutting the magazine on Grace's hand. She pretends to be in pain, which causes our group to laugh out loud again.

"Did you know that our dance recital outfits are powder blue this year?"

"Really?" I say to Grace, imagining how pretty that would be. I pull out a small bottle of moisturizer and squirt a little in my hand.

"You would look amazing in one." Grace grabs the moisturizer.

I smile, picturing myself in a dance outfit. I loved that stuff.

But I can't imagine having time for anything else with my schedule right now.

"Quiet!" Mr. Ludwig yells from behind his desk, interrupting my thought. He surveys the room. "How many groups are done with the analysis?" he asks.

Not one student raises a hand.

"If he keeps stressing out, his bald spot is going to turn the color of his nose." Sadie snickers.

Ludwig glances at the clock above the door. "Ten more minutes."

Since Ludwig always bluffs, I open up the magazine and find an article listing the best junior tennis players in the world. I scan for familiar names, knowing mine won't be one of them.

"So now that you and Maggie are doubles partners, does that mean you're going to dress like her and hang out at skate parks?" Sadie asks, dabbing my coconut lotion on her palm.

"Doubt it," I say, running my finger down the list of names and stopping on Lola Finnergin, a girl from Santa Monica who I used to play when I was younger. She's ranked ninety-ninth in the world now.

"Can you imagine Bella in a Red Bull cap?" Sadie says.

Next to the rankings is an article about Lola and her year at the IMG Bolletierri Tennis Academy. It's my dream to attend a tennis school in Florida like Lola, far away from Maggie. When I flip the page, an article on Venus and Serena Williams stares back at me. I shut the magazine.

"I think she'd look super cute in Vans and a sideways hat," Grace jokes.

"Duh," Sadie says mockingly. She tosses the moisturizer at me.

My friends break out in giggles once more.

"Okay. Enough." Mr. Ludwig announces, standing up out of his chair. His striped tie is crooked. "I've been patient with you long enough, but you're clearly not taking this seriously." He clears his throat. "Everyone on your feet. You're done. Whatever you have, you'll turn in at the end of class."

I quickly scan my paper and my stomach drops further with each question. I hadn't compared my answers to Sadie and Grace's, or even looked my responses over once, which means some of what I put down could be wrong. I toss the magazine back at Sadie and attempt to quickly check my answers.

"If you're not mature enough to handle working in groups, then you're not mature enough to sit where you want. You'll all be switching seats." Ludwig crosses his arms.

Groans ring out.

"I trust you to work together—a simple and important task— yet you're more concerned with socializing."

All the students glance around expectantly as Mr. Ludwig stalks around the room, glowering at everyone's unfinished work.

Maggie looks at Ryan and smiles.

Mr. Ludwig returns to his desk and picks up his attendance book. "I guess we're going to have to revert to kindergarten rules and seat everyone by last name."

Great. Not only am I stuck with Maggie at home and at tennis, but now I'll have to sit with her during writing class too.

Ludwig walks over to the first row. "Bella Anderson," he points to the first desk.

I tidy up my binder and book pile, then head to my new seat.

"And behind Bella is Maggie Anderson." Ludwig points to the desk directly behind mine.

I drop into my chair, keeping my back toward Maggie as she takes her seat. While Ludwig finishes seating everyone, I polish my answers. Behind me, I hear Maggie still flipping through her magazine. Figures. She couldn't care less about her grades.

"Okay. Now that we have that settled"—Ludwig begins scribbling across the white board—"maybe we can concentrate on what's important."

I glance back at Maggie, who is now ripping out magazine pages and shoving them into her notebook.

"Your first assignment is what I'm calling our audience project," Ludwig says. He stops writing on the board for a second to look at the class.

I gently pull a loose piece of notebook paper out of my binder and begin to take notes.

"I had you analyze these books because you're going to work in pairs to develop a picture book for a child, four to six years old. The purpose of the project is to first research your audience and then create an age-appropriate book based on what you've learned about childhood development. You will have to do real research—not just on your mobile devices. You'll have to visit something called *the library*."

Ignoring Ludwig's sarcasm, I point to Grace then back at me to signal our partnership for the project.

She nods and smiles.

This won't be too bad. At least Grace sits across from me and I'll get to work with her.

I scribble notes as Ludwig drones on. "We'll begin brainstorming with partners today. Remember, this project will be worth half of your grade. In other words, if you goof around and blow it off, you'll fail."

I swallow hard.

"And since we had such a hard time working together earlier this morning, I'm going to ask you to work with—" He scans the room.

My desk scrapes against the floor as I move it toward Grace.

"Let's see." Ludwig walks my way. "One. Two." Ludwig points to Maggie and me. "You will work together. And one, two . . ." He walks by us doling out numbers.

No. Not Maggie. Not again.

I look over to Grace, who juts her bottom lip out.

I shake my head. This has got to be the worst first week of school ever. It even surpasses seventh grade when I had the stomach flu.

I remind myself to picture something happy, like Joe says to do when negative thoughts impact my attitude. And just like that I picture a perfect tennis shot.

Maggie looks up from her magazine. "What did Ludwig just say?"

My mental image of a superlative tennis shot disappears. Instead, I picture myself strangling my sister.

Chapter Seven
MAGGIE

Bella lets out a snotty sigh in front of me. Then she takes a loud breath like she always does when she's stressed out. "Do you ever listen?" she snaps.

"I was busy finding stuff for my new collage." I playfully poke her with my pencil. "What's your problem?"

She just grunts. Then she places her anally organized binder on her lap.

"So what do we have to do again?" I ask, squinting at the notes on the board. Ludwig is nuts. It's only the second week of school and we already have a huge project.

"*We*? You are doing nothing. You're working with me, remember?"

"Do you think I *want* to work with you?" I fire back like I'm returning a tennis ball.

"Actually, I bet you do, because you won't have to lift a finger this way." She opens up her binder and unlatches a few pieces of paper. "Like always."

"What is that supposed to mean?" I ask, squeezing my pencil.

"I said"—she's louder now as she straightens her papers into a neat pile—"you probably won't have to do any of the work on this project since you're working with me."

"Whatever." I glance at Ryan. He's paired up with that clone Lauren from the tennis team. Ryan looks over at us, ignoring Lauren who's writing in her notebook with a bedazzled pen. I'm sure he hears everything my sister is spewing. When I make eye contact with him, he shakes his head as if to say, *You're really going to take that?*

"Look." I poke Bella with my pencil again.

"Stop messing with me while I'm writing," she whines, grabbing my pencil and tossing it at me.

"The only reason you'll be doing all the work is because you're super-controlling and you won't *let* me do anything."

"Really? That's your comeback?" she scoffs. "Why don't you just sit back and read your silly magazine and figure out what you're going to do next while I do all the brainstorming?"

"My magazines are not silly and I won't do that," I say. I point to the picture of Cory Coffey, performing a back flip on her bike, pasted on my binder. "In fact, the amazing Cory was the first woman—"

"Okay. Okay. Your BMX magazines are super-serious and school-appropriate. Therefore, you should definitely take over this project, which counts for half our first quarter grade." She pauses. "Or not."

"Just because I blew off some stupid tests in middle school doesn't mean that I'm not capable of handling Ludwig's assignment."

"Those 'stupid tests' are called finals, Maggie."

"Whatever. I still got all Bs and Cs."

"And one D."

"Math doesn't count."

"I, meanwhile, got all As," Bella says like it settles the debate.

I roll my eyes. "Chasing a perfect GPA isn't the most important thing in the world."

Bella stops writing for a moment, holding her pencil still above the paper. "Proves my point. I'm more responsible with schoolwork."

"Proves my point that you're boring."

Bella ignores me and writes.

"So what's this project about, anyway?" I ask.

She continues to ignore me.

So I stand up.

My sister looks at me. "What are you doing?"

I place my hands on my hips. "I'm going to go ask Ryan about the project since you won't answer me."

"Sit down, Mags." She points to my chair with her pencil.

I do, reluctantly.

Bella starts to explain the directions, and I sneak a peek at Ryan again. Lauren is already working so feverishly that her bedazzled pen is sparkling like a firecracker, though I can't help but wonder what she's *really* writing. Probably something like "I heart Brandon Teisch" or "I wonder what happens when people *aren't* staring at me." Fortunately, Ryan glances over at me and Bella, which is enough to draw my attention away from Lauren's scribblings. I smile at him and he gives me a hang ten sign. Then, he sticks out his tongue all goofy and laughs out loud.

So do I.

Bella clears her throat. "Maggie, I was talking to you."

"Sorry."

"And I'm supposed to let you work on this project? First off, you're not even listening to me. And second"—she points to the scraps of paper peeking out from my folder—"you can't even handle keeping your papers organized, and it's, like, the second week of school."

"This might look like a mess to you, but chaos feeds my creativity. I know exactly where everything is," I say.

"You think?"

"Just because I don't live my life like you doesn't mean I'm a slob."

Bella rolls her eyes and looks at the clock. "Okay. Enough of this back and forth. We're wasting time. Here's what we're doing. We're going to create a picture book about a girl who plays tennis."

"Uh, maybe I don't want to write about tennis." I look to Ryan again. Lauren is facing him now, yapping on and on, and Ryan is attempting to look interested.

I face my sister again. "I'm half of this group, and I have some other ideas."

"Believe me, you won't be writing the story. I will."

"Sure, Mom."

"Stop it, Maggie." She continues to scribble in her binder.

"Why can't I write the story?"

"Because."

"Because *why*?"

Bella looks up from writing and glances at the clock again.

"Look, I'll write the book and you can draw *some* of the pictures, okay? But we have to get moving. I have practice today and then a session at the club—"

"Only if I get a say in what the book's about."

"Fine." Bella rolls her eyes. "Go ahead."

"I want it to be about BMX." I hate how whiny I sound right now, but whenever I'm around Bella, things always become so unfair and I can't help complaining.

My sister lets out another loud sigh. "Mags, we can't write about BMX." She scrunches her nose. "Plus, you'll be onto something else by the time the book is due."

I feel my face heat up. "How could you say that?"

"I'm not getting into another debate with you. It's bad enough that we have to somehow figure out a way to get along to play doubles."

"Speaking of tennis, what were you and your clone friends saying about me earlier?" My voice quivers slightly. I clear my throat so my sister doesn't pick up on it.

"Look, can't we just get started?" she asks, ignoring my question.

"No. I'm not doing anything until we decide *together* what this project is about. I'm not going to let you just take over like you always do. I want to have a say."

"Seriously, Mags? You're going to pick now to act interested? Why don't you save that for tennis practice?"

"The book is going to be about BMX."

"It can't be."

"Then incorporate BMX into the book somehow. I think it's

important that kids realize they're not boxed into mainstream sports. They can try all sorts of things."

Bella presses her pencil to her paper and shakes her head.

I cast a quick glance at Ryan again, who is staring at us. He leans back in his chair and crosses his arms.

I push on the desk and stand up. "You're not even listening to me."

"Maggie, sit down!" Bella scans the room, looking embarrassed.

"No. You need to listen to me." I shove Bella's shoulder.

"Maggie, stop. Don't touch my shoulder. You'll mess up my tennis!"

I push her again.

"Stop!"

"You can shove 'your' tennis up your . . ." I shove her again. But my foot hits the desk leg and I trip, ending up on top of her.

"Get off me!" Bella shouts, waving her arms at me.

By now, a crowd has formed around us. Ludwig pushes through it. "Stop it this instant!"

Ludwig shoves his arm between us, forcing me to let go of Bella's sweater. "Both of you to the dean's office now!" Ludwig yells and points to the door.

"You're ruining my life!" Bella shouts. Her face is beet red, blotchy, and tearstained. She stomps ahead of me, leaving me standing next to Ludwig.

"You ruined mine a long time ago," I whisper, slowly following her out of the classroom. Hot tears press against the back of my eyes.

Chapter Eight

BELLA

I've never been inside the administration office before except to run an errand for a teacher. And now, because of Maggie, here I am waiting to receive my punishment for one of the most horrible offenses ever: fighting in school.

I deep breathe in an attempt to relax, but it's impossible. I'm so humiliated that when we came in, I couldn't even bear to make eye contact with the secretary who is now busy answering phone calls and typing away at her computer.

What does the secretary think of me fighting like a barbarian? What will my parents think? Worse, what will Coach Kasinski think?

This is the most awful day ever—of what's beginning to look like the most awful school year ever.

And it's all Maggie's fault.

My sister—the reason for all my misery—is resting comfortably on the leather seat across from me like she's lounging on the beach. She's so relaxed her eyes are even shut.

"How can you sleep at a time like this?" I whisper.

She opens her eyes, looks at the ceiling, and doesn't answer me.

I should have never fallen for Coach Kasinski's speech that playing together would be a good thing. She just doesn't know what Maggie's like.

"Bella and Maggie Anderson?" Dean Stewart opens the door to her office. She's sleek and toned, wearing a jacket with the Beachwood Academy insignia on the lapel.

I stand up like a soldier. Maggie, on the other hand, slowly rises, stretching like a lazy cat.

"Come on in, you two." She opens the door to her office and motions for us to be seated on two brown leather chairs in front of a large cherry wood desk that takes up half the room. The office's décor—a mix of burgundy and black—matches my mood.

I carefully drop the ice bag I'd been holding against my shoulder in the trash can and sit down dutifully, crossing my legs at the ankle and folding my hands on my lap. I straighten up and attempt to give my best innocent expression. After what feels like hours, Maggie plunks into the chair beside me.

The dean opens the two thin folders in front of her. I swallow hard when I see the form she's scanning. It's my permanent record.

Maggie yawns again beside me.

"Well, ladies, I was hoping I would meet the two of you on the tennis courts instead of in my office."

Oh my God. My hands begin to tremble. "I'm sorry," I whisper. *Just please don't tell Coach.*

"Ms. Kasinski has been bragging about her new varsity doubles team and was just telling me how talented the two of you are and how you complement each other in such a unique way. The academy had high hopes for you both this season." She lowers her glasses to the bridge of her nose.

I swallow hard.

"You know that we have a zero-tolerance policy for physical violence here at Beachwood. It is not acceptable under any circumstances."

"I'm, I, I'm . . ." I stutter.

"Whatever you were fighting about must have been very important if you decided to carry it into school like you did."

The words rush out of my mouth. "I'm so sorry, Dean Stewart," I say. I doubt Maggie is even listening. "Maggie and I were having a family disagreement that got a little out of hand. We should not have carried it over into school, as you said, and I apologize for that." I clear my throat. "I promise this will never happen again."

Maggie is too busy pulling at the strings on her hoodie to say anything. I push my ivory cardigan sleeves up my arms—I'm not sure if it's hot in here or if it's just me. I catch sight of a framed picture sitting in the center of a bookshelf behind the dean. It's a photo of her surrounded by last year's championship tennis team. I guess she likes winning as much as I do.

"A shoving match in the middle of writing class?" Dean Stewart shakes her head. She reaches into an open desk drawer and pulls out two pink forms, which I'm assuming are used for disciplinary purposes.

Maggie opens her mouth to say something, but I cut her off. "My sister and I are very sorry. I've never, ever been in trouble in all my years in school. I've never even been in the dean's office." I can feel my breath grow irregular and wonder if I should just throw Maggie under the bus by telling Dean Stewart what really happened. She should be the one getting in trouble. *She's* the one who picked on *me*.

"Well, there is a first time for everything." Dean Stewart watches me intently as if attempting to figure me out. "But both of you signed a contract a mere week ago stating that you would never engage in such behavior." She pulls out the signed honor code contracts from our folders and places them in front of us. "I expect more out of our student athletes. From what Coach Kasinski says, you're poised to take the interscholastic tennis world by storm."

I lean over to look at the signed contracts, while Maggie, who is now chewing the end of her hood's string, stares at the ceiling.

"Maggie, do you have anything to say for yourself?" The dean surveys my sister, her eyebrows raised.

Maggie's eyes dart back and forth, landing on me. I can tell she's hoping that I'll say something in her defense. When I don't, she shrugs and says, "Sorry?"

"You two are *athletes* at Beachwood Academy. This is not middle school anymore. Behavior like this will not be tolerated."

"Dean Stewart?" The secretary's voice booms from a speaker on the dean's phone.

It startles me so much that I practically fall out of my chair.

"Yes?" the dean answers.

"You're needed in the cafeteria immediately."

79

"I'll be there in two minutes," she says and pushes a button on her office phone.

Dean Stewart looks at us again before standing up. "Well, ladies, it looks like we're done here." She quickly scribbles across both forms, then holds them out to us.

My whole body is sweating now. What is our punishment? No tennis? Suspension? Detention? The possibilities are endless. I'm so screwed. We broke the contract!

The dean, who clearly already grasps the dynamic of our twin-ship, passes both copies to me. I reluctantly grasp them. I can't look. I can't look. "Once again, I apologize from the bottom of my heart," I say.

"Please have these signed by your parents."

I peek at the form, too nervous to read it.

"Since it's the first infraction for both of you and this is only the second week of school, consider this a warning. But next time—and I hope there won't be a next time—you're suspended. Per the contract. Understand?"

I nod and stare at the paper in my hand. It shakes like a frond in the wind.

"Right now, I'd strongly suggest you spend some time in my office and work out your differences before returning to class." She crosses her arms and pulls open the door. "I hope I'll be seeing you on the courts from now on—not in here."

"Absolutely," I say. "This won't—"

The door clicks shut before I can finish.

I let out the breath I didn't realize I'd been holding. "What were you thinking?" I shout as I turn to my sister, letting go of the anger pent up inside me. "This is all your fault!"

Maggie leans closer to the dean's desk as if she's searching for something.

"Mom and Dad are going to kill us. And if Coach finds out, we'll probably be kicked off the team." The hair stands up on the back of my neck at the thought.

Maggie lets go of her hoodie string and reaches for the folder on the desk. The one that contains our permanent records.

When I see her flip open the folder, I snatch it from her hands. "What the heck are you doing? We're in enough trouble already."

"Don't you want to see what's in there?" She smiles mischievously.

"You can't look at your permanent record."

"It has my name on it." She reaches for the folder again.

I move it before she can grab it. "It's against the rules." I take a few more deep breaths. "Not that you care about rules—or anything else for that matter!"

"Yes I do."

"If you cared, we wouldn't be in here!" I growl, beyond frustrated. "The dean said we have to work out our differences and all you want to do is peruse your folder. This is exactly what I'm talking about. You don't listen to anyone. You don't do what you're supposed to do."

"*Peruse*?" Maggie sighs and gives up on the folder. She saunters over to the other side of the desk.

"Maggie, please."

She picks up the picture frame with the tennis team. "Relax,

Bells. Dean Stewart is never going to suspend us. She's obviously a huge tennis fan." She holds up the picture I spotted earlier.

"Did you pay any attention to her lecture? We signed contracts saying that we would never fight in school. Contracts are legally binding."

She rolls her eyes, running her hand over the picture frame.

"What were you thinking, fighting in class?"

"You started it," she says, placing the frame back on the desk.

"How did I start it?"

Maggie walks back to my side of the desk. "I'm just tired of you being in charge of everything all the time."

"Well, then maybe you can explain to me why that's been fine for the past fifteen years, but now all of a sudden, it's a problem. And then tell me why this summer you were cool with me. And now, you're out to ruin my life."

"Summer is the only time when you're semi-normal." She folds up the pink form, lifts the back of her oversized hoodie, and shoves the form into the back pocket of her skinny jeans.

"What's that supposed to mean?"

Maggie begins to talk, but I don't hear her because outside the office the bell rings. Who is going to remember to snag my books from class? And homework. I didn't even get to transfer the homework into my iPad. Plus, I lost all this time stuck in here. Now, I'm going to have to skip lunch and work on my homework in the library so I can work out after practice.

"Hello?" Maggie says.

"What?" I answer.

"You weren't even listening to what I was just saying."

"Yes, I was," I lie.

"Yeah right. I bet you were worrying about your perfect little binder and your books and probably homework," Maggie says, leaning against the desk. "That's what you're thinking right now, isn't it? How can I get my stuff without someone messing it up? How will I ever get my homework done? And how do I make things right with my sister like Dean Stewart told me to even though I can't stand her?" She nods, pleased with herself, a twinkle forming in her eyes. She mimics me: "And what about Coach K? Oh yes. I must inform the supreme ruler of tennis of this incident before she thinks less of me." Maggie dramatically wipes her forehead with the back of her hand, mocking me. "I'm *so* stressed out."

"That's not what I was thinking," I lie again.

"Anyway. What I was saying was, you're not as crazy during the summer. You're not obsessed with school and tennis. You're quasi-relaxed and your whole existence isn't wrapped around your rankings, grades, and whatever else you're constantly stressing over. Basically, they're the only two months out of the year when you're just a little bit less of a perfectionist. It's the only time I can sort of stand you."

"I am not a perfectionist," I say, crossing my arms. "I just like to do things well."

"What are you trying to prove anyway?" Maggie picks up another photo from the bookshelf and studies it.

"I have plenty to prove." *Wait, that came out wrong.* "I mean, I don't have anything to prove."

"I knew you would say that, Bells."

I watch as Maggie returns the frame and then takes a pen from the dean's apple pencil holder. "What are you doing?"

She drops it.

I sit up straighter. "I'm not going to let you turn this back on me. You're the one who got us into this mess." I stand up. "What you see as me being a perfectionist is me actually *caring* about something."

Maggie's eyes narrow into slits. "You think I don't care?"

"No, I don't. You're constantly changing your mind about hobbies, about boys, about everything! You'll dump Ryan and be on to something new by"—I look up at the clock and see it's almost fourth period—"five o'clock today."

"That's so not true!" Maggie's hands ball up into fists.

"I can't do this with you anymore. I have stuff to do today. Stuff that I *care* about." I throw up my hands, unable to stand it in here any longer. I have three minutes until the late bell—three minutes to get my things and write down my homework. Plus, I have to talk to Mr. Ludwig and Coach so they realize I wasn't part of all this and don't think of me as some lunatic fighter. I can't waste my time in here.

I storm out of the office, leaving Maggie by herself. As I rush back to my creative writing classroom, I'm surprised to find Maggie's question replaying in my head: What am I trying to prove?

Chapter Nine
MAGGIE

Ping.

I pull the pillow off my head and feel for the clock on my night-stand, accidentally grabbing a sock instead. I toss the sock on the floor and reach again. My hand finds the clock and I turn it to face me, my tired eyes making out a glowing twelve and two zeros. Midnight? Seriously? I place the pillow over my head again.

Ping.

After a four-hour tennis practice and an hour-long lecture from my parents, I'm too wiped to get up. Screw the pinging.

Ping.

I toss my pillow on the floor and flip over from my stomach to my back. I stare at the glow-in-the-dark stars on my ceiling, will-ing myself to stand up. I might as well be up and about now since I won't exactly be leaving my room during the daylight hours. After my parents found out about the in-class smack down, they grounded Bella and me for two full weeks.

Ping.

I flip down my tie-dyed comforter, stare at my window, and stretch.

Ping.

"Okay, okay, I'm coming," I say out loud.

I stand up and step over my book bag and the discarded clothing scattered across my floor. I peek out my bedroom door and across the short hall to Bella's immaculately kept, personality-free room. The glow from her reading light creeps out from underneath her half-open door.

Ping.

I shut my door and turn around. My parents may have grounded me, but they never said anything about checking to see who's throwing pebbles at my window.

I pass my cluttered desk and the box marked "Maggie: Tennis," which I dragged out of my closet earlier before I passed out. A couple of old trophies rest against my desk drawer, along with an open scrapbook my grandma made for Bella and me a few years ago.

I unlatch my window and peer over the sill. Ryan is standing on our wooden deck. His Haro bike leans against our giant magnolia tree. Beyond the tree, a rocky bluff extends toward the ocean and provides a sweeping view of nearby Pepperdine University's campus.

Ryan's face lights up when he sees me. "Rapunzel! Rapunzel! Let down your hair!" he jokes.

"You're so romantic," I say, gathering my long brown hair into a messy bun.

"Or should I say, Sharapova, Sharapova, let down your hair?"

"You think she's hot?"

"Not as hot as you." He smiles mischievously.

My cheeks warm like they always do around Ryan. "What makes me so lucky tonight?" I ask.

"Didn't you get my texts?" He drops the tiny stones he was using to pelt my window.

"So, is this what happens when I silence my phone to go to sleep?" I ask. "You show up and throw rocks at my window?"

"No. This is what happens when my girl misses out on a serious bike sesh and doesn't return my texts." His voice grows louder with each word.

"Shh . . ." I say. "I'm in trouble enough as it is."

"Aw. Are you grounded because of the whoop-ass today?" Ryan looks up at me with his baby blues—the ones I can never seem to get enough of. "The whole school's talking about what a kick-ass fighter my girlfriend is."

"Yup," I whisper, not sure if I should be pleased that people are impressed with me or annoyed by what got their attention.

"Come on. Just climb down the tree. I'm sure all the Andersons are fast asleep by now."

I look over my shoulder at my closed door and then at my bed. "Wait one second," I whisper. I rush toward my bed, shove all my pillows underneath the comforter, then pull the blanket over them to make it look like I'm asleep in case someone decides to check on me.

I yank a pair of baggy jeans over my pajama shorts, grab my hoodie and hat off the floor, and shove my feet into my slip-on Vans.

Then I carefully climb out the window opening and stretch my foot toward the rough bark of the magnolia. Once I'm stable, I push off the windowsill and hug a huge limb. I carefully climb down the rest of the way like the tree's a ladder, using the branches as rungs.

"Whoa. You really are amazing," Ryan says once I reach the last branch. He moves his bike to make room for my landing.

Once my Vans hit the deck, Ryan wraps his arms around me.

He buries his face in my neck. His hot breath sends shivers down my back. The drip-drop-drip of the fountain my father just installed on our deck gives the whole thing a kind of movie quality, as if the water is the soundtrack to our reunion.

I kiss his soft lips.

"I missed this last week," he mumbles.

I wrap my arms around his waist, leaning my head against his chest and breathing in his crisp scent. "Me too." I listen to his heartbeat and stare out at the mountains. Lights from houses below pepper the coastline like stars. I shut my eyes, enjoying the feeling of his chest against mine.

"How long?" Ryan asks after a few minutes.

"Huh?"

"Your punishment."

I look up. His black knit hat is pulled low near his eyes, just as I like it. "Oh, that. Two weeks."

"Suckage," Ryan says a little too loudly.

"Shh . . ." I hold my finger up to his full lips. "It's going to be eternity if I get caught out here. You know how my parents are about obeying orders. That's why they love Bella so much."

"Was it worth it?" Ryan asks. He pulls me behind the back fence of the practice tennis court my parents installed for Bella last year.

"I don't know." I kick a rock. It puffs dry dirt and lands against a cactus. "I was just pissed that she wouldn't listen to me."

"Yeah, I could tell. Is that where you were after practice? Getting grounded?" Ryan asks.

"Yeah. Sorry about that," I say, cringing when I sit down on the cool, dry grass. My butt is still super-sore from tennis.

"So are you suspended too?" Ryan asks, falling to the ground next to me.

"We got off with a warning."

"A warning? That's awesome. My buddy Mark got suspended and all he did was bang into someone a few days ago."

"Was Mark on the tennis team?"

Ryan looks at me from the corner of his eye and smirks, show-ing off the sweet dimple on his right cheek. "Nah. He wrestles."

"It seems Dean Stewart is one heck of a tennis fan." I stare out at the waxing moon.

"Maybe she's hoping you two will use that anger on the courts."

"Let's hope not since the only person I seem to be fighting lately is my doubles partner." I twist my head his way again.

He wraps his arm around my shoulders and begins massaging them. I'm more comfortable right now than I was in my bed a few minutes ago.

Bells thinks that I move from guy to guy. She doesn't get it. The other guys meant nothing; most of them were just friends. It's dif-ferent with Ryan.

He leans in and kisses the back of my neck. "Did you miss it?" he whispers in my ear, sending shivers down my stiff legs.

I'm so wrapped up in how awesome it feels to be with him—in this one moment—that I don't hear his question.

"Mags, did you?" He gently nudges my cheek so that I'm facing him directly.

"Wait—what?"

"Did you miss playing tennis?" He nuzzles in so that we're nose to nose. "You talked about having a master plan and everything"— after Bella left the skate park the other night, I ended up giving Ryan all the gory details about how I want to prove everyone else wrong about me—"but I dunno . . . the way your sister's getting to you and stuff, I just have to ask."

"No, uh . . . uh, no." I struggle for the words. "What I miss is, umm, riding with you guys. I hate that I didn't get to squeeze in some time at the park today."

Ryan grins at that one, his smile so large that it seems to spread to his now glimmering eyes. "Yeah, that's the Mags I know." He places a hand on each of my shoulders, shaking me playfully. "A bunch of us snuck out tonight. We found a great spot off Trancas Canyon to ride," he says excitedly. "That's why I'm here. To pick you up."

"And cut out of my punishment?"

"Wouldn't be the first time you snuck out to ride." Ryan shrugs.

I stand up and brush the dirt off my jeans. "I *am* due for some BMX."

Ryan grabs his bike. "Cool. You ready?"

"Just give me a sec to grab my bike." I walk along the fence of our court toward the garage, catching sight of a tennis ball stuck in the chain link. It seems to stare back at me.

If I get caught sneaking out, my parents will definitely pull me from the tennis team and I'll miss my shot at proving to everyone that I'm more than Bella the Great's irresponsible sister.

I can't risk it.

"Sorry," I say, stopping at the ball in the fence. I turn around reluctantly and face my boyfriend. "I can't go tonight."

Ryan reaches out, grabs my hand, and pulls me closer to him. "You sure?"

It's hard to say no when his closeness is so enticing. I look up at Bella's window, still glowing from her reading light. "Yeah. I have tennis tomorrow and I'm already in trouble. If I go, my parents will flip out and I probably won't be able to see the light of day until winter break."

"Tennis, huh?" He smirks again. "So I was right. It's more than just a thing, you know, to show your family that you're serious about stuff, isn't it?"

"It's, uh"—the thought comes unsolicited: it's a thing I'm really good at, maybe the thing I'm best at—"it's nothing." I let go of his hand and kiss him on his chilly cheek. "What I'm worried about is, umm . . . not being allowed out of the house to ride with you guys. It's just not worth ruining everything for one night." I opt for a half-truth.

"You *sure* you don't want to go? I'm trying out my 360 tonight on these hills that are shaped like two quarters."

"Positive." I give Ryan another quick kiss and run to the tree, launching myself back up before he changes my mind. When I look down, he's still staring up at me, checking to see that I'm all right.

I wave to him once I'm inside my bedroom, and he blows me a dramatic kiss. Then he mounts his bike and takes off.

I turn around and kick a sock on my floor, frustrated that I can't go with him. For a second, I think I see the light under my room flicker, like someone's standing at my door. But when I swing the door open, no one's there.

I plop down on my bed and resign myself to a night spent alone.

Chapter Ten

BELLA

Thwack.

At tennis practice the next day, I serve another ball Maggie's way and wipe the sweat off my face with a pink wristband.

Maggie mocks my anticipatory foot bounce. She returns the ball with a two-handed backhand, a giant smile plastered across her face. "Hee!" she screams. Ever since walking into the family room while I was watching some of the pros at the US Open this weekend, she's been imitating the sounds they make hitting a ball. She says it helps with her rhythm. Please.

The ball tips the net and I jump forward, chipping it back to Maggie's side. She backhands the ball over the net again, and I run the ball down. Spotting an opening, I poke it past her. "Yes." I pump my fist.

Maggie flashes another bright smile at me. Is she actually enjoying this? I thought she just decided to try out for tennis to torture me? I want to believe that she's being genuine, but if she is, then why did I see her climbing out her window to be with Ryan last night?

"Ready?" I ask my sister. At least today, she finally wore proper tennis attire. Well, sort of proper: a tank and a gray pair of guys' mesh tennis shorts.

Maggie nods. She bounces on the balls of her feet, her smile wider than the doubles court. It was her idea to play against each other instead of opposite Lauren and Minka, and clearly she's pleased with the result.

I bounce the ball twice. Then, I toss it into the air and wind back my racquet. "Ehh!" I use the serve that Joe and I refined this summer and launch a ball Maggie's way.

"Nice serve, Bella!" Sadie, back from the conditioning run, yells to me before bending over and touching her toes.

Maggie returns the ball with her booming forehand. "Hee," she grunts.

"Get it, Bella!" another teammate yells. I don't look for fear of missing the ball, but it seems like a bunch of them have begun to congregate around our court.

I sprint to the ball and forehand it back toward my sister. *Take that, Maggie.* This is my court and my sport.

"Nice, Bella!" Sadie cheers, standing near the baseline.

Maggie confidently attacks the net, lobbing the ball back to me.

Before the ball dies a slow death, I sprint to it and slice it so that it spins over the net. My heart races with excitement. There's no way she's going to be able to hit that one back.

Or so I think . . .

Somehow Maggie gets to the ball before it meets the court and sends it over the net again. "Yes!" I hear her say.

"Uh," I yell, backhanding the ball to the open spot on her weak side. *Right back at ya, Maggie.* Finesse wins every time.

"You go, Bella!" Sadie shouts.

"Hee!" Maggie sticks out her racquet over her head. Her form is ugly, but she somehow gets it back to me.

Thwack.

The yellow ball bounces right in front of me. I pull my racquet back and take a side step to slice it. This time the ball spins tight. I'm confident that once it bounces, my sister will misjudge it. She just doesn't have the experience to judge a topspin like mine; that slice won me the July 4th Singles Tournament at the Santa Monica Tennis Club.

"Nice slice, Bella!" someone else yells. The crowd of teammates gathered around the court to watch our sisterly brawl is growing by the minute.

"Hee!" Maggie grunts, smacking the ball back to me.

So much for the spin. Maggie's explosive energy lets her get to anything.

Sweat rolls down my back. The ball bounces high, and I spot my opportunity for a power shot. I wind my racquet back, calling on a level of adrenaline I usually save for tournament finals.

Twhack.

I smash it toward Maggie.

She rushes to the well-executed shot and manages to make contact, sending the ball behind me and out of bounds.

"Yes!" I pump my fist again.

The crowd bursts into cheers.

"Yay! Bella!" Sadie screams.

"Way to go!" a teammate chants.

Maggie looks at me, pointing. "Bring it on, sista!"

I shake her off, grabbing another ball from the metal basket. "What, and beat you again? Haven't you had enough?"

"I said, bring it on," Maggie says, swaying from side to side in her ready stance.

I haven't seen Maggie this determined to beat me since we were twelve, before her infamous assault on Joe's nose. Maggie and I used to play each other like this for hours; only then, we always passed a small brass cup back and forth to the winner as a kind of pseudo trophy.

"Another point, Bella. 30-15. You got this game!" Sadie shouts.

I toss the ball into the air, and it seems to hang there suspended for a moment.

Thwack. I hit it.

Maggie forehands the ball back to me. I don't even have to move. I return the ball with my two-handed backhand, adding a bit of spin. I've got this. She is so done.

Maggie's still unfazed. She hits one over the net with her forehand.

I'm about to run to get it when Coach Kasinski bursts out of her office, her eyes narrowed and her cheeks red with anger. "What is going on?" she demands. I freeze at the baseline. The tennis ball bounces and smacks the bleachers behind me.

Maggie raises her hands in victory.

I glare at my sister.

Sadie stands beside me at attention along with our other team-mates who gathered to watch me and Maggie do battle. I can hear a few gulps among the crowd. A couple girls even look down at their feet.

"You two were supposed to play Lauren and Minka while the singles players were conditioning!" Coach shouts. "You're not sup-posed to be playing each other!"

Lauren and Minka look up from playing calmly together at the court adjacent to ours. Lauren catches the volley from Minka. "We totally asked them to but they insisted on playing each other," Lauren offers, happy to add some more fuel to Coach's fire.

"Uh huh," Minka drawls, pushing out her plump lips.

"Liars," Maggie snaps.

"Maggie!" I shout.

When Coach isn't looking, Maggie sticks her tongue—*yes, her tongue*—out at Lauren.

I shake my head at my sister.

"How are you two going to learn to play doubles if you don't practice as a pair?" Coach's eyes dart back and forth between me and Maggie. I stare at my Nikes and tap the racquet beam against my toe. Two reprimands in two days is more than enough trouble for me.

But apparently not for Maggie. "Isn't that kind of hard, *Coach K*?"

I look up to see Maggie smile mischievously. *Oh no. Don't do it, Mags.* I hug my racquet to my chest and bite the inside of my mouth.

Coach snaps at her. "Excuse me?"

"You know, isn't it kind of hard to play like a fruit? How exactly do you do that?" Maggie puts on an innocent face.

Sadie snickers.

We're so dead.

"Wait," Minka says, squinting her eyes. "What is she talking about?"

Lauren shrugs.

One of our teammates whispers, "Like a pear. It's a pun."

"You have gone too far this time, Maggie Anderson!" Coach Kasinski yells, slamming her clipboard on the court. "First, I stuck my neck out for you by giving you a spot on this team. Then I had to explain to the dean why two of my tennis players were fighting in class. And now, I step out of my office to find you and your sister messing around instead of working together." She takes a deep breath as if to calm herself down; it doesn't work. "And you have the audacity to talk back to me?" Coach's voice rises with each syllable as she charges toward my sister like a bull.

"I'm sorry—" I begin to say in Maggie's defense. I can't bear to have another authority figure mad at us because of my sister's big mouth.

Maggie shrugs, keeping eye contact with Coach the entire time.

Coach either doesn't hear me or chooses to ignore my words. "We're only a week away from the start of the season. You are a *doubles* team. And you're playing like you're about to win a state singles title against *each other*!"

"I'm sor—" I say.

"Not another word!" Coach turns around and shakes her long index finger at me. "You're both putting yourselves before the team—placing this franchise's dynasty at risk. You should be ashamed of yourselves."

I take a huge gulp of air.

"And, Maggie!" Coach Kasinski steps back and points at my sister's shorts. "Don't even show up on my courts again without gender-appropriate tennis attire. Do I make myself clear?"

"Yes, ma'am," she says, with a fake Southern twang.

Coach begins to walk away, muttering loud enough that we can hear. "And to think that I thought you both had a chance to qualify for the California Classic. Please!" She bends down and picks up her discarded clipboard. "If you don't learn to work together," she says more distinctly, "you'll never win a tennis match, much less anything else."

I reluctantly walk to the other side of the net to show Coach that we're unified, but once again tears sting my eyes because of Maggie. I should have never let her convince me to play singles against each other. She'd begged and pleaded, saying that it'd be more fun and that Lauren and Minka were total airheads. I didn't want to make a scene by fighting with her yet again, so I gave in. Big mistake. I really should have stood my ground. I would never, ever, put my team in jeopardy. Maggie might be making a joke out of the season, but tennis means everything to me.

Coach turns to Sadie and the others. "As for the rest of you: another round of conditioning for taking part in Maggie and Bella's assault against team unity. Utterly disgusting behavior for this team, this franchise, this school to engage in."

Groans ring out from a few girls.

"Complain and it will be two sets of conditioning."

Silence sets in. I drop my racquet and begin to run with the rest of the team.

"And take the A-course!" Coach shouts.

More low groans rumble. The A-course is the steepest and the most difficult conditioning trail. It runs up steep hills and through the nearby canyons.

"This is so unfair," Lauren huffs behind me a few minutes later.

"Tell me about it," Minka says next to her.

"I hate running the canyon," Lauren whines. "Brandon says that they *never* have to do this in his surfing club."

Minka rolls her eyes at her. "Laur, stop making excuses. Lately you hate working out at all." Then she catches up to me, her voice taking on a more deprecating tone. "And to think . . . Bella's biggest weakness is her own sister. What a joke." She takes off in front of me, pumping her lean tan legs.

Next to me, Maggie's face turns pink. "Shut up, clone," she shouts at Minka's back.

Here she goes again.

"Maggie!" I snap at her. The last thing I need is problems with our teammates. "Just stop it."

Minka turns around and scans my sister like she would a designer knock off. "Nice shorts." She snorts derisively. Minka and Lauren catch up with the rest of the leaders.

"You only wish—" Maggie starts.

"Will you just . . . stop?" I look at Maggie. "Please!"

"But—"

"It's one thing if you want to run your mouth and ruin your own life, but stop ruining mine."

I take off to catch up with the other girls, the ones who actually take tennis seriously and aren't here to ruin it for everyone else.

"But—" I hear my sister behind me and run even faster.

I wish Maggie would just quit.

Chapter Eleven
MAGGIE

At the end of practice, Coach K glowers at me. Then, she shakes her head like my mom does when I bring home anything less than an A on my report card, which—let's face it—is most of the time. When she's done attempting to make me feel small, she walks into her office.

"Whatever." I shrug it off and swing my bag over my shoulder. If only we had a normal coach, like Joe, who is still globe trotting to tennis clinics, this season would be so much better.

I charge ahead and frantically look for Bella in the locker room, but there's no sign of her anywhere. The only person left is Bella's clone friend, Sadie, digging through her tennis bag frantically searching for something.

"Have you seen Bella?" I ask her.

Sadie ignores me. She stands up and grabs her bag. A B-Dub ID card is in her hand, which probably means that she's taking the school bus. I can't think of another explanation for why she would have pulled it out at the end of the day. I try to hide my surprise—all the "tennies" I've ever met are filthy rich. When she realizes I spotted the pass, she hastily shoves it into the side pocket of her bag, confirming my suspicions.

"Hello?" I say again. With her tiny nose stud, dyed black hair, and heavy eyeliner, she looks more Venice than Malibu. I start to wonder if she's not like the other clones. That is, until she opens her mouth.

"What's your deal, anyway?" she snaps, tilting her head to the side. Her turquoise eyes shine as she twirls a piece of black hair around her index finger.

"What are you talking about?" My bag falls off my shoulder.

"Are you trying to ruin all this for Bella?"

"Huh?" I ask, shaking my head. "Why would I want to ruin anything for her?"

"You kinda are though. First the fight in class, and then today getting Coach all fired up. What's that about?"

Why does this girl care? From what Bells says, she doesn't even care that much about tennis. But, then again, Bella thinks no one cares about tennis as much as she does.

Sadie lets go of her hair. "It certainly seems like you're trying to make her life miserable. Just saying."

"Uh, did you miss our practice match today? Because if you saw how well we played against Lauren and Minka *after* we ran the A-course, you'd realize I'm actually *helping* Bella," I say, adjusting my bag and pushing open the door I came through. "Just saying."

I leave Sadie in my dust and run down the hallway, passing glass trophy cases overstuffed with Beachwood accolades. I exit through the double doors to the parking lot and am shocked to see Ryan on his bike. He's using the curb to practice his feebles.

"Hey," he says once he spots me. "All done?"

"What are you doing here?" I'm caught off guard for a moment. Ryan usually heads straight to the skate park after school.

"I figured since you're punished, this is the only way I can catch some time with my superstar tennis vixen."

I scan the parking lot.

"You're so busy, Masha, I hardly ever see you anymore." Ryan pinches my side.

I meet his eyes and smile at his Sharapova reference. Then I catch sight of Bella behind him, about to climb into Grace's black Beemer. "I'll be right back," I say and dash after her. "Bella, wait!" I yell. Within seconds, I'm at Grace's passenger door. "I need to talk to you."

Bella doesn't look at me. Her face, red and blotchy, points straight ahead. "Just go," she says to Grace in a monotone.

Grace peels out of the spot.

"Wait!" I shout, jogging after the car. My legs are as heavy as cement from all that conditioning—which admittedly I caused.

When Grace's car is out of sight, I return to the curb and sit. Defeated, I bury my head in my hands.

"Rough day?" Ryan cuts his bike next to me, causing his tire to rub. He leaves a black skid mark on Beachwood's pristine white concrete.

I peek up at him. "What on earth gave you that idea?"

"What happened now?" he asks. "Another sister smackdown?"

I hang my head again. "Not exactly," I mumble into my sore forearm.

"Still got it all under control?"

"Yeah. Sure."

"You think?"

"I *know*." I stare out at the almost empty parking lot as the dusky sky grows darker.

"This will flip your mood," Ryan says, taking off.

I look up as he pedals full speed toward a rocky hill about four feet high at the end of the sidewalk. "Ryan, what are you doing—" I yell to him. But I'm too late.

He rides fast up the steep incline. Then, he launches himself into the air. Once he's airborne, he yanks his bike to the side, spinning his handlebars and completing a barspin. He lands on the other side of the mound with a thud, missing a tree by mere inches.

I let out the breath I was holding and try to relax—to feel at ease like I did while I was playing Bella. Before Coach K threw a hissy fit and messed everything up again.

Ryan turns around and pedals on the sidewalk, using his feet as brakes to stop in front of me.

"You're crazy."

"The only thing I'm crazy about is you!" He ruffles my sweat-stiffened ponytail.

I look up at him as he hops off his bike and leans down to rub my shoulders. "It's nice to see you smile again," he says.

We lock eyes and Ryan pecks me on my lips upside down like Spiderman.

I giggle when our lips touch. But I can't get too comfortable—

images of Bella's face before she peeled out of the lot fill my mind. I have to talk to her soon.

"Nice shorts," he says, letting go of my shoulders and climbing back on his bike.

"You like?" I stand and pull on the sides.

"Yeah. They're hot," he says, squeezing his handlebars.

"I think you're the only one who likes them," I say. "Coach K says I have to put on a skort or I'm officially off the team."

"Can't wait to see that," he snickers.

"Ugh. I know. Can you imagine me in a skort?"

"You'll look good no matter what you wear."

"I swore I'd never wear a skort again," I say wistfully, skipping along the curb.

Ryan raises his eyebrows at me. "Sounds like there's a lot you're doing lately that you swore you'd never do."

"Yeah, I guess . . ." I mutter.

"Then, quit," he says, matter-of-factly. "Tennis, I mean."

"Yeah. Right. That's exactly what my sister and everyone else expects me to do. I have to follow through with my plan."

"Ah . . . the master plan. How's that working for you?"

"Well, besides the skort, Coach K being a wicked witch, and the fact that my sister won't talk to me right now, it's actually going great," I say. "Really. To tell you the truth, I forgot how much I like tennis."

"I guess I'm just not a fan of all that varsity stuff. It's all so bogus. It's just a chance for parents to clap and say they're good parents because their kid made the team or scored a goal or earned a trophy."

Ryan rides his bike in circles in front of me. "Sports should be about just going out there and doing your thing."

"You know I'm with you on that." I think about how when I'm on the court being myself, I do have fun . . . as long as Coach K isn't there and my sister is acting semi-normal.

"I still don't get it. You're going to put yourself through all this just to prove something to your parents?"

"It's for me too. I'm really enjoying playing." I sit and lean my hands on the cool concrete, shutting my eyes. "I even kind of miss the competition part—the satisfaction of winning. And, you know, I'm actually pretty good." *As good as you are when you're riding*, I think.

Ryan stands on his back pegs and jumps the curb sideways. "Doesn't surprise me that you've still got it, but are you having as much fun as you do at the skate park?"

I shrug. "Yeah." I want to tell him more. Like how sometimes I have even more fun on the court. "I guess I forgot how much joy I get out of beating clones on the court. One of the many perks of tennis."

Ryan chuckles. "You missed a sick time riding the trails last night."

"I'll be back riding all the time as soon as tennis season is over."

"Yeah. Until your family talks you into playing year-round."

"Trust me. No way I'm turning into Bella. But it would be nice to win something this season. Something big," I say, shocking myself.

I'm watching Ryan balance on his back pegs when a wave of anxiety rushes over me. I have to go. Now. "Look, Ry, don't worry about me." I walk over and quickly kiss him on his sweaty cheek. "I know exactly what I'm doing."

"If you say so, babe." He smiles at me.

"I do," I reply, grinning back. "Catch you later."

I walk the dirt path home, formulating a plan. Coach K was right about one thing. With my power and Bella's finesse and experience, we are pretty amazing. If we could just find a way to work together, we could definitely kick some major butt.

Chapter Twelve
BELLA

Lying on my bed with my laptop, I do my nightly scan of the names of the top thousand USTA junior tennis players in the world.

I read through, sigh, and click out of the site. Then I go to YouTube and bring up my favorite Wimbledon final matchup between Serena and Venus Williams for a pick me up. I study the clip intently as they play each other with such force and grace.

That's how I want to play.

When the match highlights are over, I look on the sidebar for another video to watch. Thinking back to the article I read in *Tennishead*, I reluctantly click on a Venus and Serena doubles match.

Venus and Serena are amazing on their own, but as a pair, they are untouchable. I can't imagine how their opponents felt when Venus poached the net with her lethal speed and power while Serena used her finesse and touch to repeatedly place the ball deep in the back court.

Coach Kasinski's words ring in my ears: *With Maggie's power and your finesse* . . . I click on a YouTube video that Dad posted a few years ago of a young Maggie and me playing. I can hear Joe's voice in the background as Maggie, like Venus, returns a serve using her powerful forehand. The ball is hit deep to me, and like Serena, I naturally slice the ball back over the net.

The tennis world had such high hopes for us. Could we still prove it right?

I remind myself that Maggie quit. And she'll quit again unless I do something about it.

I shut my laptop.

There's no use in trying to convince my sister to keep playing. I may as well just speed up the process and get her to leave tennis before she makes things even worse for me. But how?

She likes to surf. Maybe I can convince her to join the swim team. Do I still have the flyer they gave out during orientation last spring? That might get her to switch. Especially since it's coed.

I pop off my bed and stand in front of my desk, staring at the tennis trophies and ribbons that line the shelves around my pastel pink room. I carefully open my bottom desk drawer. Next to a partitioned box filled with carefully organized old dance memorabilia is an official Beachwood Academy royal blue folder. I open it and flip through the contents. The swim team pamphlet is tucked behind the left portfolio pocket. Perfect.

I put the folder back, and before shutting the drawer, I run my hands over the pink and purple ribbons from my dance days. Tons of warm fuzzy memories flood my head as I think back to my first recital and the euphoric feeling of performing in front of an audience.

I catch the sweet scent of a preserved flower bundle from inside the drawer and lift it to find a picture of Maggie and me. I pick it up and stare: Maggie, in her denim overalls with scuffed knees, and me, in my black tutu with the multicolored leotard—both of us toothless with our arms wrapped around each other and smiling wide.

I reach for my planner and jot down a quick idea for the picture book.

It had to be my ride home with Grace that brought on all these sentimental feelings about dance. All she did was rave about the dance company at school and how much I'm missing out by playing tennis all the time.

Grace just doesn't get it.

My phone alarm signals I have forty-five minutes until a practice match at the club against one of Joe's clients. *Oh my God.* I just wasted a full fifteen minutes thinking about Maggie. Once again, she impedes on my life.

"Will you open the door?" Maggie shouts from the hallway, as if she's read my thoughts. She wrestles with the locked doorknob. "You're being ridiculous. I just need to talk to you."

I open up the homework file on my laptop and disconnect my Wi-Fi so I won't be distracted by the Internet. "I'm busy."

The doorknob jiggles. "Come on, Bells. Just give me five minutes."

"I told you—" Suddenly, I remember the swim pamphlet. I swing open the door to find Maggie standing there in sloppy sweats and a baggy tee. "Hi," I say sweetly, holding the pamphlet up for her to see.

She eyes the pamphlet quizzically, then barges in and hands me the small brass cup we used to give each other when one of us won a match.

"Huh?" I say, utterly bewildered. I'd just thought of the trophy today.

"You won today. It's yours," Maggie says, collapsing on my bed.

I run my hand over the cup. Even though I haven't seen it in more than three years, a bazillion memories flood my head. I had no idea she kept it.

Shutting the door behind her, I place the cup next to my laptop and straighten out the wrinkles Maggie just caused on my bedspread.

I've wasted enough time today on memories.

She scoots up to the headboard, dragging her sheepskin boots across my chenille bedspread. "Look, Bells, we have to talk."

"Gross." I point to her chestnut-colored Uggs.

"Seriously? I barely wear these outside." Maggie rolls her eyes, pulls off the boots, and tosses them across the room. "You're so anal."

"I have something for you." I ignore her attempt to pull me into another argument and hold out the only reason I allowed her into my bedroom.

"What's this?" she asks, taking the pamphlet. "I saw you trying to give it to me before."

"The swim team. I think you should try out." I point to the pictures. "It looks like fun and from what I heard it's a great opportunity to really showcase how dedicated you are—"

"Just hear me out before you try to trick me into quitting tennis." She tosses the pamphlet on the floor. Orange Gatorade stains the corners of her mouth. I can just see her opening our fridge and drinking it straight from the bottle.

"Out, Mags." I pick up the pamphlet and Maggie's boots and place both tidily outside my door.

"I know you're pissed at me because of the whole Coach being angry thing, not to mention writing class the other day, but just listen. I really have something important to say about tennis."

I'm vaguely curious what Maggie would consider important, but not enough to forgo my schedule. "Out." I point to my door.

"Please." Maggie looks up at me with her baby blues imploringly.

I'm reminded of the time when I was sick with a stomach bug the first week of seventh grade. Mom and Dad were busy with a big divorce case and left me home with the housekeeper. That morning, Maggie opted to skip school and take care of me, holding back my hair and doing the things parents should. I tend to take care of the big stuff, but Maggie takes care of me when I need it most. "What is it?" I sigh.

Never one to sit still for even a second, Maggie scoots to the edge of the bed. "Okay, here's what I'm thinking. If we show Coach K that we can beat Lauren and Minka, we can snag the number one slot."

"What?" I'm officially perplexed. Is this why Maggie joined the team? To steal thunder from the girls she calls clones?

"Yeah. We can do it," she says, mimicking Rob Schneider's character in *The Waterboy*.

"That's crazy," I say. "Come on, Mags. I have to finish my homework. You need to get out."

"No, you need to listen to me."

I fall into my desk chair, exhausted by Maggie's nagging. "Explain to me how we can possibly beat Lauren and Minka? They're the number one doubles pair at Beachwood and they're one of the best Junior doubles pairs in the country. They're older than us, and they're the freaking co-captains—they're way more experienced than me or you, especially you, since you quit!" I yell the last word.

"So?" Maggie bounces off the bed. "You saw us out there today. We almost beat them in the second set."

"They were probably just tired from all the conditioning, or maybe they weren't really trying because they didn't think they needed to. It was a fluke."

"It wasn't a fluke. We're good, Bells. Good enough to beat them. Why don't you believe that?"

"Because you haven't played an actual tennis match since the sixth grade! That's why."

"It doesn't matter." Maggie shrugs.

I stare at my sister. "Regardless of your grand ideas, Maggie, Coach will never change the rotation until Lauren graduates. They're the defending champions."

"Coach K said herself she thinks we can beat them. You heard her. The first day she met me. At the club. She said we could be better than them," Maggie says eagerly. Then, mocking Coach's firm tone, she sagely adds, "They plateaued."

"Not if you—"

Maggie holds up her hand. "First off, Coach K is psychotic. But I'm willing to give in a little, so I'll work on my mouth, and I'll even grab one of your stupid skorts to wear tomorrow." She rolls her eyes.

"You're going to wear a skort?" I look at her in disbelief.

She nods and bites her bottom lip. "Yeah, but don't think that means that I'm suddenly going to start buying skirts or dresses. It's not happening. I'll never wear anything uber girly. And I don't see how you . . ."

I tune out Maggie's babbling. *If she's slapping on a skort again, then she has to be serious.*

"So if you don't think Coach of the Year will let us play Lauren and Minka for the number one spot on the team, then we should try to enter that tournament thingamajig she mentioned," Maggie says.

I perk up. "You mean the California Classic?"

"Yeah," Maggie replies. She sits on the edge of the bed, bouncing up and down.

"Coach Kasinski has to enter us, so I wouldn't get your hopes up there, Mags." She rolls her eyes, and I continue, shaking my head. "You know, you're not exactly setting the world on fire with her lately. I can't see her doing us any favors in the near future."

"Details." Maggie pretends to yawn.

"Important details," I confirm, still staring at my sister. *Why is she so hell-bent on tennis all of a sudden?*

"Come on! Did you hear the way Minka talked to you today at practice? Are we just going to take that from her? From both of them?" Maggie launches herself off the bed, bounding over to the lounge chair I set up in front of the picture window that looks out on the cliffs that stretch toward Pacific Coast Highway.

"Sure, Lauren and Minka can be a bit too much to handle sometimes." I bend down and straighten the rug corner she just kicked up. "But they wouldn't even be saying anything to me if you hadn't showed up at tryouts."

"So?"

"Honestly, you've irritated a lot of girls. You haven't played in years and now you're one-half of the number two doubles pair."

Maggie stretches out her arms and pulls a neatly folded afghan off my window ledge and curls up beneath it. "Exactly."

I roll my eyes and cross my arms like our mom does sometimes. "I just don't get you."

"What? That I'm not a control freak like you?"

"Don't try to pull me into another debate with you right now. The fact is that Lauren and Minka are just irritated with you, as are the rest of the girls." I pull the afghan up to Maggie's shoulders so that it's not touching the floor. "You showed up. You barely have any competitive tennis experience. And you mouth off every chance you get, landing extra conditioning for everybody. What do you expect?"

"You don't see what I'm saying." Maggie sits up and leans forward, messing up the blanket once more. "Whenever somebody new shows up at the park, nobody pays attention to them unless they can ride. If they're decent, they get killed. And if they're amazing, that's when they really get a hard time. The fact is, no one cares if you suck."

I grab my lucky racquet from a bag inside my walk-in closet. No more wasting time chatting with Maggie. I have to head out back to practice.

"Don't you get it?" Maggie says. "Lauren and Minka think we're good. Maybe even better than them. That's why they're being all nasty."

I take a deep breath. "Say they do think that—so what?"

"You're telling me you're just going to accept that Minka and Lauren are the best, let them bust on you, and you're not even going to challenge them? Just because they're older and walk around like divas who own the place doesn't mean they're better than us. In my humble opinion, Lauren is lazy—and burned out. And I realize I didn't know her before, but I think it's gotten worse since she started dating the slacker, Brandon."

"You also have a boyfriend, remember?" I raise my left eyebrow. "What makes Lauren different?"

"I get the sense that she's kind of using him as a crutch, you know? Just an excuse not to do things."

"I dunno . . ." I mutter. "How can we really know what their relationship is like? Maybe they're soulmates?"

"And your point is?" Maggie replies, deadpan.

"My point is that sometimes it's not worth it to make a fuss."

"And sometimes it is!" Maggie presses.

I shake my head. "Tennis is different. There's a ranking system that dictates seeds in tournaments—you can't just barge in and challenge a top player—you have to earn the right to the match."

"Who cares? All the more reason to beat them." Maggie has that look on her face, the one that she always gets when she's determined to prove someone wrong about her. "We have the advantage, Bells. One, because I'm a lefty with a strong forehand and you're a righty with an awesome backhand. And two, we're twins. We practically read each other's minds."

I sigh. If we somehow managed to beat the O'Donnell girls, it would catapult my tennis career into the next stratosphere. But that would mean Maggie sticking with tennis for more than a minute, which, considering her past, is a long shot. But I'll bite. "So do you have a plan?"

Maggie raises her eyebrows conspiratorially—clearly, this is the question she's been waiting for all along. She proceeds to gesture wildly and rattle off strategies for beating Lauren and Minka—how we should combine my right with her left to hit angles and cut off opponents' shots with our court coverage, how we can probably tire Lauren out, how we can pit the two against each other. She's precise and detailed for once, and I think back to the YouTube video of Venus and Serena. Maybe we can pull this off.

But then I deflate, plopping down on my bed, my racquet in hand. Maggie is no Venus. "Are you sure this isn't some sort of sick way of getting back at me?"

Maggie sits up straighter. "What? No! First Sadie, now you."

"What about Sadie?"

"Oh, you know. She thinks I'm out to get you."

I think back to what Grace said in English class. "Did she say that you resent me for always being the center of attention, because of tennis and school, and that you feel down on yourself because you know you could be just as good if you only worked as hard as I do at stuff?"

"Uh, let's skip the psychoanalysis." She stares off for a second, jutting her lip out. I know she's deep in thought. That's the thing about twins; she can't hide anything from me.

"You swear you're being genuine and not just leading me on?" I stare at her, attempting to put the puzzle pieces together.

"I'm sorry that I've been screwing up royally lately. But trust me, I really want to prove to everyone that we can do it." There's a glimmer in her eyes. "I really like tennis. I always have." She looks down.

I walk over to my sister, carefully placing my racquet on the ground. "Pinky-swear that this is for real?" I stick out my pinky finger like we used to back when that photo of us—grinning and toothless—was taken.

"One condition. You have to hear me out on the picture book."

"Fine," I say, willing to sacrifice the picture book if it means she'll take tennis seriously.

"Okay then. Pinky-swear." My sister wraps her matching pinky around mine.

"Then let's start practicing," I say. "You can come with me to training tonight, and we'll have Mom and Dad fill out the paperwork to get you back into the USTA. We might have to play in some local tournaments to—"

"Ugh! Another practice?" Maggie falls back on my bed. "We just had a four-hour one."

"Maggie, you promised!"

"Just messing with you!" She pops up and busts out laughing so hard she falls on my pink carpet right on my lucky racquet.

"Mags!" I shout, falling on the ground next to her. "My racquet!"

She digs it out from underneath her. "You mean this?" She holds up my purple Head. "It's time for a rematch! Race you to the court." She grabs the cup, dashes out of my room, and flies down the steps.

"Wait!" I call out. "I've got to text the club to tell them I'll be late!" I frantically type in the message, then grab another racquet from my tennis bag and take off behind my sister, scrambling to make up for her head start. By the time I've reached the court in the backyard, Maggie's placed the brass cup next to the net.

"This one is for the cup," she announces. "And Coach K isn't here to mess it up."

"You're on!" I shout.

Maggie spins the racquet's grip between her palms in anticipation. I toss the ball into the air and whack it.

My sister returns the ball with her left-handed forehand. "That cup is mine," she shouts, giggling.

"Fat chance." I hit the ball with my backhand. A burst of energy shoots through my body, so strong that it surprises me.

Maggie attacks the net and challenges me with a drop shot, her lips turned up in the biggest smile I've seen in a long time.

"I don't think so." I run up to the ball and lob it over my sister's head, positively overflowing with joy. I don't know whether Maggie's intentions are true or whether she's got some crazy plan to get back at me or whether we'll actually be able to beat Lauren and Minka and make it to the California Classic. All I know is that there's nowhere else I'd rather be at this moment.

And for now, that's enough.

Chapter Thirteen
MAGGIE

"Out."

"Tennis balls," I mutter as my fifth flubbed serve hits just beyond the service line. Bella nods at me encouragingly as I grab a ball from the pocket of my ebony skort (yes, I'm wearing it and I hate it more than brussels sprouts). I bounce the ball once on the court and twice on the back of my calloused hand for good luck. Then I toss it into the air and wind up my racquet. "Hee!" I yell as I somehow get the ball to the other side.

The Oakcrest player on the deuce side returns the serve with a strong forehand.

"Out. That's game," Bella calls. She points to the yellow ball as it bounces just outside the baseline.

In our first official doubles match, Bella and I are up 30–love— terminology which I've never understood, by the way. Why is love worth nothing? Love should be worth forty at least.

Speaking of love, Ryan is here. But I don't have a second to think about that kind of love right now.

"Do it again, Maggie!" Bella slaps me on the back and steps up to the service line. She fixes the Oakcrest player with an intense stare, like if we don't win, the world will cease to exist.

I stand behind the baseline and pull out another ball from my skort as the Oakcrest girls glare at me like they want to devour me. Then I complete my lucky bounces and toss the ball into the air. "Hee!" I shout, hitting a sharp serve to the tall redhead from Oakcrest. The ball hits just inside the ad box.

The redhead returns the serve but it puts her momentarily out of position, causing Oakcrest to mis-hit the ball.

Thwack.

Bella anticipates the shot and chases the ball down in the doubles alley. She backhands it over the net.

The redhead attacks the short ball and smacks a backhand.

I explode into a run and forehand the ball back over the net. "Hee!" I shout, using the grunt to help with my timing.

God, I love this.

Oakcrest returns the ball.

"Ehh," my sister, always in perfect position, cries as she smacks the ball across the court.

Immediately, Oakcrest's blondie responds with a perfectly executed baseline stroke.

I bounce on my feet and wind up.

"Got it!" Bella yells behind me.

I step aside to give her a chance to backhand the ball. This is the kind of stuff we've been working on since our talk: using signals and callouts to work together instead of against each other. Suffice it to say, so far it's working.

"Eh," Bella reaches out with her racquet and backhands the ball to the redhead.

She poaches the ball and sends it back to me.

I sprint to the ball and hold my racquet straight just like Coach K showed me. Just before I hit it, I can't help but flick my wrist a bit to give the ball a little extra zing, even though Coach has lectured me a million times about technique. I end up shanking it, and the ball bounces hard into the net instead of where I intended it to go.

Coach K drops her clipboard to summon my attention from the sidelines. When we make eye contact, she hardens her gaze and points to her hand on a racquet, modeling the correct form I failed to apply.

Bella turns around and nods at Coach to show her agreement. Then, she looks at me. "Yeah, Mags. Continental grip."

Whatever. Since I'm in it to win it, I politely nod in Coach K's direction. Unfortunately, she doesn't take my nod as an act of respect. Instead, she adjusts her position on the bench and crosses her arms tightly across her chest, a pose that I've learned is her "mad stance" after witnessing it at least a dozen times within the past few days.

I can't do anything right when it comes to that woman.

"30–15," I say as I grab three balls from the wire bucket. I tuck two balls under my skort and hold one out.

Tap. Tap. I bounce the ball twice off the back of my hand, then once on the court. In my mind, I hear Joe's words from a few years back, mixed in with some snippets of self-advice: *A serve is just like throwing a football. No big deal. No more unforced errors, especially on* big points. *I'm older now. What happened at the last tournament I played won't happen today. It's just a game. Don't act like Bella.*

My nerves flutter as I toss the ball into the air and wind up my racquet behind me.

Thwack.

The ball bounces in the diagonal box.

The Oakcrest player with the red hair grunts and returns the ball toward my sister. I step toward it, attempting to hit it back, but I feel my sister going for it so I stop mid-stride. "Mine!" she calls out. Once again, in perfect position, Bella hits another smooth backhand.

The blond smacks a light lob that bounces my way. This one juts high and I can't remember if I should smash it or hit a lob to change up the pace.

"You got it!" Bella yells.

I lightly lob the ball back over the net, deciding to go with safety instead of my usual strategy—instinct.

Redhead uses the high bounce as an opportunity to wind up for a smash.

Oh no.

I watch in horror as the ball sharply bounces Bella's way. She hits a beautiful passing shot for the point.

Man, she's good.

I turn to my sister and hold my hand up for a high five. "Oh yeah!" I yell as we slap hands. I add a butt-tap with my racquet for kicks.

"Smash it next time," Bella says. "Kat can dish out the smash, but she can't handle it."

"You know these girls?" I ask.

"Don't you remember them?"

"Uh. No." Even when we were young, Bella was always insistent on knowing everything about who we were playing. I preferred just to show up and play. As far as I was concerned, if it wasn't Venus and Serena standing on the other side of the court, then the girls were beatable. Why bother knowing who they were?

She turns around. "That's Kat," she points to the redhead. "And that's Megan. They played singles at the July 4th tournament. Kat has a power serve and Megan is quicker than Minka. They're not great, but they can get hot and really wreck a draw. I've seen them take down top seeds in early rounds."

I nod in understanding. "Game plan?" I ask.

"Attack Megan's weak side and come to the net more."

As I'm jogging back to my spot behind the baseline, Coach K shouts at me again. "Maggie, use your hustle!"

No kidding.

I nod Coach K's way as Bella turns around and mouths the score to me again so I don't have to figure it out on my own.

"40–15," I mumble, spinning my racquet between my palms. With shaky hands, I pull another ball out of my skort for the serve. I haven't felt butterflies like this since the last tournament, and everyone in the world knows how that one ended.

Stop thinking about that tournament.

I complete the lucky bounce—two off the top of my hand and one on the ground. Here goes nothing. I toss the ball into the air and miscalculate the contact.

Dong.

The ball hits the fence behind Oakcrest. "Fault" the receiver yells loud enough for people three courts down to hear. Nearby players look at each other and smile.

Great.

Bells turns around and nods at me. "You got it, Mags."

Okay, serve, you need to cooperate. Again, I do my lucky bounce with the ball.

Thwack.

Great. Double fault.

"40–30. Match point," I squeak.

Bella turns around and signals for me to calm down. I take a deep breath. This is so embarrassing.

As I'm about to whack the ball, Coach K grabs my attention with a hand signal. When I look at her, she's squeezing the tennis racquet and pointing to her temple to signal me to think. I bet she wishes she was gripping my neck instead of the racquet.

"Fault," Kat yells as she moves out of the way. She smirks at Megan.

Coach K claps swiftly. "Come on!"

Bella jogs up to me. "No worries. You can do it. Don't think. Just hit the ball," she says, then turns around and jogs back to her spot. Before she sets up, she freezes as if she senses my tension. Then, she turns around again and mouths, "Just have fun."

Really? Bella telling me not to think? To just have fun? I laugh out loud at the irony as I toss the ball into the air for the serve.

Thwack.

This time the ball bounces inside the box.

I exhale.

Kat smacks it back to me.

I lunge at the ball and chip it just over the net to her backhand.

"Eh!" Megan runs down the ball but misjudges the bounce and shanks it.

"Yes! Match!" I pump my fists and hold my hands up in the air. Bella runs by, tapping my butt with her racquet. Then she grabs the scorecard from the net. "Nice job, Maggie."

"Wait. No handshake?"

Bella tilts her head and smiles. She holds out her hand and we complete our celebratory shake—two back and forth hand slaps, a shake, and some finger-wiggling pizzazz at the end. We used to do this back in the day to celebrate one of us winning a competitive match.

"Booyah!" I shout when we finish.

Bella giggles and shakes her head at me. "Come on. We have to shake hands at the net."

I nod and follow her. As we're waiting for the other team, Coach K walks up to us. She snatches the scorecard from Bella. "Save the excessive celebration for when you actually win a title. You're a Beachwood tennis player, not someone from some no-name school. Act like you've been here before."

I bite my bottom lip to remind myself not to mouth off to this monster.

She continues to storm across the court toward Lauren and Minka's match like we just lost and should have something to be sorry for.

Bella lowers her head. Then, she shuts her eyes and slowly inhales.

"She's crazy," I say after we shake hands with the Oakcrest players.

"We're lucky she's our coach. Girls would die to play for Beachwood." Bella pats me on the back.

I flare my nostrils. "Umm . . . with her? I don't know about that."

She shakes her head at me and charges ahead toward the bench.

"Well, at least we're one down," I say to my sister when I catch up, trying to lighten the mood once more.

She puts down her racquet, starts digging in her tennis bag, and doesn't respond.

"I can see us beating Lauren and Minka already!" I prod. I grab my sweats. Even though the sun is warm, I can't wait to pull on pants to hide this silly skort.

"Maggie, it was our first real match of the season." She picks up her bag and slings it over her shoulder.

"Exactly. And we killed it."

"Not to burst your bubble, but in the grand scheme of things, this win means nothing," she says, almost like she's trying to channel Coach K.

"Yeah, well, I can't wait to beat the crap out of Lauren and Minka and become the number one team. Those girls—"

"I really hope you're not doing this because of some personal vendetta." Bella again shuts her eyes and inhales deeply. "Lauren and Minka are two of the best tennis players in the country. Yeah, they're prima donnas sometimes, but they're our teammates."

I shrug. "Then, after we beat them, we can show them where to shove their trophies."

Bella looks around furtively. "Shh! Maggie, think. The last thing we need is some reporter hearing about a tiff on the Beachwood Tennis Team. The tennis world is tight knit and tiny."

"Hey Maggie! You coming?" yells a familiar voice.

I look up at the stands and see Ryan standing there, holding an In-N-Out bag. He winks at me. "Sweet!" I exclaim, pumping my fist.

Bella looks up to match my gaze. "Burgers after a match? Maggie, you should be eating—"

"I told you I'd take this seriously, but I'm not turning psycho," I say.

"Your diet—"

"Think of it as refueling with lots of iron. Want some?"

"No thanks, Mags. I have to prep for my singles match."

"Wait," I say to my sister. "What's the deal with love?"

"Huh?" Bella grabs her racquet.

"Why is it worth zero? Don't you think that's wrong? It should be worth way more."

"Seriously, Mags? Is that what you think about when you're out there playing?" Bella shakes her head.

I shrug. "Uh, yeah."

She rolls her eyes, then begins walking toward the court for her singles match. Suddenly, she stops mid-stride, turning on her heel. "I almost forgot, Mags. Nice job." She gives me a thumbs-up.

I smile to myself, then sprint up the stands.

Chapter Fourteen
BELLA

Two weeks, nine doubles wins, and six singles sweeps later, I'm in a fabulous mood.

Grace and I are going over our creative writing homework before Ludwig gets to class. "Can you just take a look at this and let me know if anything sticks out to you?" I show Grace my story-boards. For a second, I remember what Maggie said once about how my life is all about stats—my grade point average, tennis rankings, body fat index, serve speed, etcetera.

"Watch the comma splice here," Grace says, using her purple pen to circle my work. "Other than that, it looks good to me."

"Thanks," I say, making another notation on my paper.

"Hey, congratulations on all the wins lately." Grace sits up straight and untwists the hair band around her ponytail. Her flaxen waves flow freely over her shoulders.

"Thanks." I glance over at Lauren, who's standing in the doorway talking loudly on the phone, probably to her boyfriend. It occurs to me that maybe Maggie had a point about Lauren's looking for ways to slack off.

"I'm assuming stuff is going better with your sister then?"

"Actually, yeah. It's been great." I watch as Maggie and Ryan wiggle past Lauren, Ryan's arm wrapped around my sister's shoulder as they walk into class. Ryan pulls Maggie into a hug and kisses her cheek. Maggie beams.

"You okay?" Grace asks, staring at me.

"Of course." I snap my head in Grace's direction. "How's dance?" I ask.

"We have our first rehearsal tonight for the fall show," Grace says, clapping her hands swiftly.

"Awesome," I say, anxiously checking the clock. I remind myself to transfer my homework to my iPad and then figure out how to get it done before training.

"I'm seriously psyched. It's an amazing performance and we pulled it off so quickly."

"What are you guys planning on doing?"

"It's a great routine. We've combined ballet with some freestyle— like a little bit of classical mixed with old school Britney Spears."

"Nice! What music are you using?" I ask, feeling nostalgic. I think back to when I danced a solo during my last year at the studio.

"Rihanna."

"Get out!" I say. I still break out in a few old moves sometimes when I overhear Maggie's music while I'm doing homework in my room.

"You know it." Grace puts her hands up and shimmies like she's on stage.

"Are you performing at school?"

"Yeah, in the auditorium—on the new stage they just installed. You should see it. The floor was built with a little bit of bounce and everything. Just for our routines." She pauses. Then her face lights up like mine does when I win a point. "We usually practice at night. Maybe you could join us—you know, if you're done with tennis in time."

"Can't." I cut her off before she goes on any longer. It's no use. I look at the clock.

"If you can't join, you should at least come check out the rehearsal tonight—get a peek at the big show before we go on for real in a few days."

"No, really—"

Grace cuts me off. "I'd love to hear what you think about the routine. You always had such an eye for choreography."

"You think?" Grace is such a great dancer—I always looked up to her. I had no idea she thought highly of me too.

"Madame Henderson was so sad when you left. She always said you were such a natural." Grace adjusts her heather gray half cami over her violet tank.

"Really?"

"Yeah! You should definitely stop by. Our dress rehearsal starts at seven—in the auditorium."

"Okay, sure," I give in. I have a ton to do, but Coach did give us a bye-day today because she has a meeting. I could probably squeeze in a few minutes between conditioning and homework to stop by the rehearsal.

"Yay!" Grace claps.

"Okay, class. Take your seats." Mr. Ludwig walks in and drops his books on the front desk, startling a few students.

I scurry across the room to my seat in front of Maggie. "Guess what?" I turn around and whisper to Maggie while Ludwig is busy talking to a student in the back of the room.

"What?" she asks, rolling up the sleeves of her long-sleeved Vans shirt.

"Does anyone have any questions before I give the deadline for the picture book project?" Ludwig asks, interrupting my sister and me.

"I'll tell you in a sec," I say, turning back around to face the front. I raise my hand.

"Yes, Bella," Ludwig points at me.

"What type of book are you looking for? Fantasy? Realism? Anthropomorphic?"

"Anthro-what?" Maggie whispers behind me.

Ludwig clears his throat. "Excellent questions, Bella. I'm looking for whatever type of book you would like to write. Whatever book will tell the story and teach the lesson you're striving to teach—and most importantly, whatever book you think would be of interest to children four to six years old, based on your research."

In front of Ryan, Lauren raises her hand. "Can you go over those types of books?"

As Mr. Ludwig explains the different types of picture books, I pull out my iPad. I input the dance rehearsal into my calendar between conditioning and homework, then stare at my schedule, willing it to fit.

"Any other questions?" Mr. Ludwig asks.

I'll train after school; then I'll tackle homework. After dinner, I can run to the auditorium and then sprint back home. That way I won't feel guilty about not conditioning.

"Great. The books are due on Friday, October fifteenth. You have about a week and a half from today to finish it."

I put the assignment on my calendar. That's the day before the California Classic. It's less than two weeks away. I really shouldn't go to the rehearsal. I still don't know whether we have a spot in the Classic, but so many huge names in tennis will be there at the tournament—I can't afford not to practice in case we get selected. I delete the rehearsal, and my gaze drifts over to Grace, my thoughts turning to how Maggie would probably say I'm being really lame, even more than usual. I retype the entry into my calendar. I really want to go to support Grace and say hi to all my old friends, and I'll only stay at the rehearsal for a few minutes anyway.

Mr. Ludwig leaves us to work on our projects, and Maggie pokes me with her pencil.

"I know what we can do now for the book," she practically shouts.

"Wait. Before we talk about the book, I have to tell you what I'm doing tonight," I say, eager to prove to Maggie that I'm not always all work and no play.

"Let me guess, you're playing tennis." Maggie leans her head on her hand and pretends to yawn. "And you need me to work out with you again tonight."

"Nope." I say coyly.

Maggie sits up. "Wait—nope I don't have to go, or nope you're not playing tennis tonight?"

"Grace asked me to go to the dance rehearsal tonight! She wants me to give the group some feedback."

"That's awesome, Bells."

"Yeah, I know. I can't wait."

"What about conditioning and all that?"

"I got it all figured out," I say. "After homework, I'll run to the rehearsal—you know, run the hills—poke my head in and check out the rehearsal, and then run home."

"Of course. All planned to the second." Maggie opens her binder. "I wouldn't expect anything less."

"You want to come with me?"

"No."

I deflate for a second.

Maggie furiously flips through a jumbled pile of papers. "Now, I had the best idea for the picture book. Where did I put it?"

"Do you realize something?"

"What?" Maggie freezes.

"We're totally switching personalities right now," I say, pointing to my sister's binder.

"What do you mean?"

"You're acting all studious, and I'm ready to blow off responsibilities."

"Uh, I wouldn't go that far." Maggie stops flipping through her stuff and looks up at me. "You're just taking a few minutes to check out a rehearsal. That's called living. L-I-V-I-N-G. Normal people do it every day."

"Then why do I feel like I'm doing something wrong?" I confess, staring at my iPad.

"Because you're a perfectionist and you totally need to mellow out." She gives me a knowing look, a lopsided grin on her face.

"Whatever. And you're sloppy." I reach across the desk to grab her binder. "Let me organize that for you. It's driving me insane."

"Never!" Maggie shouts, swiping it back.

I laugh as we play tug-of-war with the binder for a minute.

Ludwig appears next to my desk. "Problem, ladies?"

"Oh," I say, looking up at him.

"No, just messing around," Maggie informs him.

"Again?" Ludwig pushes his lips tightly together.

"Sorry, we'll get right back to work," I apologize. "Seriously. We need to get started on this," I whisper to Maggie as Ludwig walks away from us to check on other groups.

"I've got it all under control," Maggie says loudly, looking over at Ryan. She pulls a few pieces of crumpled paper from her binder and smoothes them out in front of me. "So, what do you think?"

"Nice." I stare at the pencil sketches. One features a girl holding a racquet. Another is a sketch of the same girl on a bike.

"You know, I haven't seen you this excited about something in a long time," she says, watching me intently.

I look up from her sketches. "What?"

"Seeing the rehearsal. You're pretty psyched about it."

"Yeah, I guess." I flip through my binder and open up to the story I wrote last night for the picture book. When I look up, Maggie is still staring at me. I maneuver in my seat feeling uncomfortable.

"You know you can do both. Play tennis and dance."

My smile sags and I clear my throat. "No, I couldn't go back to dance. Not enough time. And besides, I love tennis."

"You could pull it off." Maggie continues to prod.

I lean my forehead on my hand, exhausted just thinking about it. "Not if I want to break through in tennis."

"What's wrong with scaling back? No one says you have to be all tennis all the time."

"I dunno . . ." I sigh, then force myself to focus on the work in front of me. "We should get moving on this project." I rest my open binder on Maggie's desk. She moves her sloppy pile of sketches to the side. "I was thinking that we could incorporate both tennis and BMX by writing about twins. Like us. You know, a memoir slash fictional story."

"Yes!" Maggie says excitedly. "That's exactly what I was thinking."

I feel someone staring from across the room and look up.

It's Lauren. "Aw . . . look at the twinnies getting all enthusiastic. Aren't they just adorbs?" Lauren says loudly.

I stiffen in my seat.

"Maybe they'll be the next Juicy Fruit twins." She cackles.

Ryan chuckles, more at Lauren than at the comment itself. He shakes his head.

"It's Doublemint, genius," Maggie shoots back at Lauren.

That makes Ryan laugh out loud. He smirks at Maggie, bugging his eyes to show what he thinks of Lauren.

"Shh!" Ludwig admonishes from the front of the room.

"Mags . . . she's our teammate," I say, looking at Lauren, who has pulled out her phone and is texting underneath her desk.

"Mr. Ludwig?" a stiff secretary voice bursts forth from the speaker.

"Yes?"

"Is Maggie Anderson there?"

"Yes she is," Mr. Ludwig replies, his eyes meeting Maggie's.

I look down at my notebook. *Great. What did my sister do now?*

"Could you please send Maggie to see Coach Kasinski at the end of class?"

"Sure."

I cross my arms. "Maggie, you swore . . ."

She shrugs. "I didn't do anything. I have no idea what Coach Kraz-inski wants to talk to me about." Maggie's eyes widen, showing me that she's telling the truth this time. That's the thing about twins. I might not be able to read her mind, but I can definitely tell when she's lying.

Chapter Fifteen

MAGGIE

"Come in and have a seat, Miss Anderson," Coach K says to me. I slowly saunter into her office, my eyes adjusting as I leave the mid-day sun outside. It's not like I'm nervous. I didn't do anything.

I pull out the chair in front of Coach K's wide desk. Over fifty trophies stand at attention like brass soldiers, while other even larger cups, prizes, and awards line the floor, surrounding the tiny office like castle columns.

"Do you know why you're here?" she asks, reclining in her black leather chair. It lets out a loud squeak.

"Um . . ." I pull my legs up to my chest to stretch out my thigh muscles, sore from tennis training.

Coach K looks over her bifocals and points to my legs. I let go of my stretch and sit correctly. She continues to peer at me as she moves her playbook and coffee mug to the side of her desk.

"Do you see this collection of trophies?" She gestures to the accolades behind her.

"Uh-huh," I say evenly. I'm not wowed by trophies. Bella has plenty and all they do is collect dust in her bedroom. Does Coach honestly think I'm in this for the trophies?

"This is what's called a dynasty. And do you know who coaches this dynasty?"

"You do," I say, knowing that this is what she wanted to hear. I cross my legs for another quick stretch. Another day. Another lecture filled with self-congratulatory rhetoric from Coach K. I stifle a yawn.

"Exactly. I'm in charge of this dynasty." Her lips form a tight line.

I stare at her gleaming porcelain coffee cup and attempt to spot my reflection.

"The way to create a dynasty is to introduce talent to good coaching. I call it the Kasinski way. Are you serious about learning tennis the Kasinski way, Maggie?"

"Sure," I say to placate her.

She stares at me with pursed lips. "I think it's great that you and Bella are winning. You both harbor a lot of talent, just as *I* recognized on the court that day I met you." She pauses, giving me a chance to let her words sink in.

I nod, wondering where this is going.

"But you're still number two."

"Actually, I was wondering about that—"

Coach K cuts me off. Her severe eyebrows rise almost to her hairline. "I don't think so! We are not here to talk about where you fit in the rotation."

"Okay." I shrug. It was worth a try.

"You think it's acceptable to ask me about your rank when you're the kind of player who wastes precious match time hanging out with a boy in the stands?" She bangs on the desk, shaking her mug and catching me off guard.

"Huh?"

"If I ever catch you with a boy while a match is still going on, you will make the team run. Do you understand me?"

I bite my bottom lip to restrain myself from rolling my eyes. *What is this, 1950?*

"Not only did I catch you in the stands socializing, but I also saw you eating greasy fast food!"

The horror.

"Do you know what greasy fast food can do to your game? I never ingested anything greasy while I was training."

Maybe you would've played better if you had, I want to say. Instead, I focus on a brass cup from 2003. If I make eye contact with this lady, there is no way I'll reign in the words that are dying to burst from my mouth.

"That's just the beginning. You have been putting forth a tad more effort, Maggie, but you continually refuse to listen to my coaching. And although you say you'll buy into the Kasinski way, your actions speak louder than your words—and they're unacceptable."

Here we go again.

"You need to listen to my instructions. I can make or break an athlete's career. You are lucky that I can spot talent and that I insist on working with the players I see promise in."

What is wrong with this woman?

Coach K leans across her desk toward me so I have no choice but to make eye contact if I look directly ahead. Instead, I avoid her gaze and concentrate on a signed poster of Maria Sharapova hovering behind her to the right. *Interesting* . . . Bella and I do kind of look like Maria with dark hair.

Coach K jabbers on. "This is my team. These are my rules. It's my way or you're out. Understand me?"

"Yes, Coach," I say. Someone should tell her that she looks like a prune when she gets angry so maybe she'll simmer down a bit.

"Well, since you don't seem to listen to me on the courts, maybe you'll do it during our special practice sessions." She settles back in her chair.

Wait. What? Extra practice?

Coach has a cruel glint in her eyes. "You are going to work with me every day after practice on some of the more basic techniques, such as your volleys, smashes, and serves, and more specifically your grip, which is causing your inconsistent shots. It's time to fully immerse you in the Kasinski way."

Ugh, I think to myself. She wants to teach me old school tennis; turn, step, and hit. Where's the creativity in that? Where's the fun?

"But—" Extra practice would be such a drag. This means I'll lose the little free time I have left.

"You have a lot of catching up to do."

"I don't think it's necessary," I try again.

She purses her lips, making that prune face again. "Like I said: there are a lot of girls who would kill for a chance to work one-on-one with me. Beachwood Academy is a legendary dynasty, and I can't take the chance of placing our reputation in jeopardy. I could certainly demote your sister to the freshman squad and kick you off the team to open up a slot for a more serious player if you think that's the better option." She leans back and crosses her arms. "Can you imagine what that would do to your sister?"

"No, we can't do that," I say, clearing my throat. This woman is so awful.

"Honestly, you are more of an annoyance than an advantage to me right now. The only reason I'm agreeing to help you is because I was the one who discovered you, and I've never seen a pair quite like you and your sister. With my coaching, you really could do amazing things for this team. I can see the headline now." Coach forms the half square with her hands again and gazes into it. "'Legendary Coach Olga Kasinski Leads Unknown Doubles Team to Victory.'" Her eyes migrate back to me. "But, if you're not dedicated, I'm sure I can—"

"I'll do it," I say, thinking about my pinky-swear with Bella, about Lauren and Minka's smugness, and about the look on our parents' faces if I don't pull through. I just wish I didn't have to work with tennis-Stalin over here.

"Good. Then I'll see you today after school. Be ready to work on your stance and serves. We have a lot to accomplish in a limited amount of time." She folds her hands across her lap, looking pleased. "Now, go." She shoos me out.

I bite my lip to keep myself from spewing what I really want to say—how I can't believe that Bells and my parents think this woman walks on water. She's nasty and out for herself. She doesn't care about me or Bella. All she cares about is her accolades.

"Go!" she shouts when she notices I'm still staring at her.

I stand up and stride to the door.

I've barely shut Coach's office door behind me before Bella is standing in front of me biting her index fingernail. "What did she say? What did you do?" Her eyes are the size of tennis balls.

"Nothing. It's fine." I keep my head down.

"Seriously. What did she say?"

"I just have to do some extra practice."

"Is that all?" Bella asks, lowering her finger from her mouth.

"*Is that all*? If I'm practicing with her, I'll never get the chance to go to the skate park."

"The skate park?"

"Yeah. Remember. The skate park? I agreed to play tennis, not marry it."

Bella lights up. "I'll go with you. We could practice together."

I turn around and stare at the royal blue door with Coach's name plastered across it in gold. "Nah. Don't worry about it."

"No, really. I'd love the extra practice."

Before I can respond, Bella is knocking on Coach K's door.

"Ready?" Coach K yells from across court later that day.

While everyone else is enjoying their bye-day (including Bella— Coach K was convinced that I put my sister up to asking to join us, and it cost me five laps), I'm still at the courts. My palms are rubbed raw, and I can think of a billion other places I'd rather be than here with her.

Coach K's white tennis skirt is wrinkled and her face shines with sweat, but she shows no sign of slowing down after a full practice.

First, she pushed me to hit over two hundred serves because according to her I suck at serving and still have miles to go.

No surprise there.

Then she forced me to use my serve to hit strategically placed cones fifty times. Finally, after three grueling hours, I thought I was done. I grabbed my water, took a sip, and shoved it into my bag. Then I said goodbye to Coach.

"Where do you think you're going?" she yelled back.

"Home."

Saying that cost me three laps before we continued the session, which she reminded me was only halfway done.

The Kasinski way is as crazy as she is.

She shouts at me now. "On to smashes. You're having such a difficult time with your serves because of your lack of technique, and that's also going to affect your smashes."

I stifle a yawn. Not because I'm bored this time—because I'm dead tired.

"When an opponent wants to lob the ball over your head for a point or position, a smash is preferred—not a volley. The purpose of the smash is to win the point or at least make it difficult for your opponent to return the ball."

I nod in my ready position as my legs shake like jelly.

She lobs the ball my way. I run under it, point at the ball with my free hand, and hit it like a serve. It sails high and smacks the stands behind Coach K.

"Remember. Relax your grip when you swing, and then wait to squeeze the handle until right before you make contact. You don't have to hit the ball hard and tight. Power comes from your lower body."

I nod, too exhausted to speak.

"Again." Coach K lobs the ball my way. I loosen my grip, then point and whip my racquet. This time the ball bounces right in front of the service line.

Thank God. This should be over soon.

"Good. Remember to utilize the continental grip." Coach K nods. Behind her, the assistant coach who's working with us tosses Coach K another ball. She looks as defeated and exhausted as I feel. "Again," says Coach.

She lobs another ball my way. I point, wind my racquet back, squeeze the grip, and smash it again. This time the ball bounces hard beside Coach K, who doesn't budge. Instead, she places her racquet in front of it like a machine, hitting the ball back to me. I run it down, but it bounces before I'm even close.

Coach K is a beast. I wonder what she could do on a bike, not that I'd ever want to find out.

"Good." She nods. "Again."

I hit twenty more smashes as the sky begins to darken. It must be at least six o'clock, which means I've been out here for at least four hours.

Coach K flips on the outdoor lights as I'm drinking from my fifth water bottle. She places red cones on the court across from me like she did while I was working on my serve three hours ago.

I re-bandage my palms, bend over breathing deeply, and begin picking up balls with the hopper. *Please be done. Please be done. Please be setting up cones for tomorrow's practice.*

"This time, I want you to hit the cones."

"What?" The word tumbles out before I can stop it. "Coach, I just did this with my serves. Don't you think—"

Coach K claps. "Enough!" She looks at the assistant, who is slowly rolling out the cart filled with balls. "Dynasties aren't made, they're earned."

I swallow and set up on my side.

"I will dismiss you after you knock over fifty cones."

"Fifty?"

"Keep talking, Ms. Anderson, and I'll make it fifty times in a row."

The assistant tosses a ball my way. I point and smash silently. I'm too exhausted to worry about my grunt. The ball darts just shy of the back left cone.

I look at Coach pleadingly.

"Fifty to go," Coach K says. She stares at me with eyes that would freeze an ocean.

An hour later, I can barely drag myself up the front steps at home. Before I open the front door, I hear the familiar *thwack* of tennis balls hitting the garage wall, followed by the sound of someone grunting.

I pull out my phone to check the time. Then I charge ahead toward the lit tennis court. With each step, my stomach sinks.

Sure enough, I find Bella hitting forehands against the side of the garage that backs up against the court. *Why is she here?* The ball ricochets back to her as she hits it over and over again with flawless motion.

When she sees me, Bella catches the ball she's swatting. "Hey,

Mags!" she says, hugging her racquet. "How was your session with *Coach K*?" She emphasizes the nickname, poking fun at me. "Did you learn a ton?"

"It sucked." I stare at the racquet in her hand. "What are you doing?"

"What do you mean what am I doing?" She grabs a white towel off the net and wipes the sweat building on her forehead. "I'm practicing." She giggles.

"You were supposed to go to the dance rehearsal," I say, staring at my sister's frozen smile.

"Oh. Yeah. That," she mutters, looking down at her racquet. She twines her fingers through the strings. "I didn't go."

"What?" I drop my bag beside me. It lands with a thud.

"I couldn't live with myself after such a short practice, especially when we're in season. So I worked out and then after I finished dinner and my homework, I came out here to work on my net game. You know, since Coach always says I'm more of a baseline player." She drops her towel on the court and runs back to her spot in front of the wall. "Wanna hit with me?"

She's back pelting shots before I can say anything. I feel the frustration rising in me, but fighting with her won't work. I have to use another angle. If I can just get her to stop for a second . . .

"Bella!" I shout.

"Yeah?" She turns around, the spotlight on her ivory skin and blue eyes making her look angelic.

"Want to help me out with something?"

"Yeah! Your serve?" she asks, excitedly. "I'd love to. Just grab your racquet and—"

"No. Something I need to talk to you about."

"I really need to work on my short game."

"I want to tell you more about the practice, specifically the . . ." I think for a second. "The smash."

Bella stops hitting for a moment and shrugs. "Okay." She follows me into the house.

Chapter Sixteen
BELLA

I trail behind Maggie into the foyer to chat strategy. As soon as we're in, she grabs my arm and swings me around to face her.

"Hey, easy!" I look down at her tight grasp on my right arm. "That's my dominant arm."

"What happened?" she asks, looking at me like she just caught me defluffing her favorite childhood teddy bear, Gumbo.

"What do you mean, what happened? I was practicing tennis. Jeesh." I pull my arm away from her grasp and rub the red marks her fingers left behind.

"You were supposed to go to Grace's rehearsal! You were so excited about it in class today and I thought . . ." Maggie stares into me like no one else can.

I look away, feeling uncomfortable, then gaze up the stairway toward my room. I should still be outside on the court. I would be, if Maggie hadn't lied about wanting to talk tennis. "Look. I really should be getting back to the court," I say, hoping this will get my sister off my back.

"Bells." Maggie sighs.

"What?" Why is Maggie making me feel so guilty? I'm just doing everything I can to be the best. What is wrong with that? What is wrong with working hard to reach a goal?

"What happened? Why didn't you go?"

I sit on a step. "I called Mom after school and told her about my plan to stop by the rehearsal."

Maggie shakes her head and looks up at the ceiling.

"She told me to stop at home before I went anywhere. So I did."

"And then that's when Mom and Dad told you it would be a better idea to work on your transition game?" Maggie says flatly. Her bottom lip juts out.

"Yeah. They didn't think it was productive to waste time at the rehearsal."

"But—" Maggie pleads.

"They're right, Mags. I should be practicing." I look away from her gaze. "And when I got home, Dad showed me the newspaper. Did you know that we were mentioned in the High School Tennis Wrap-Up? They called us the 'Anderson Aces.'" She lights up. "A number two doubles pair is never mentioned in the paper."

"So? That's a ridiculous and exaggerated alliteration, considering I can't hit an ace to save my life."

"Regardless. Do you know how long I've been waiting for this? It's not easy to get noticed." I let out an exasperated sigh. "And Mom and Dad are right. I shouldn't be wasting my time at a dance rehearsal. I should be taking advantage of this opportunity."

"You were only going to stop by the rehearsal for a couple of minutes."

"Maggie, I can't blow it now. We're so close. Mom and Dad are just trying to protect me from failure."

"And protect you from fun."

"I have fun at tennis."

"Why do you always let Mom and Dad tell you what to do?"

I use the railing to pull myself up to a stand. What does Maggie know? I've been at this for ten years *straight*. I need to get back outside to practice. I'm wasting precious time trying to justify my actions to someone who will never get it. "Because they're my parents and they know what's best for me. You should try to listen to them too. It makes life a lot easier."

"Oh yeah?" Maggie stares at me.

"Speaking of fun, were you really with Coach for five hours? I bet you were hanging out with Ryan." I put my hand on my hip.

"I wish! I was working out with that monster of a coach." Her eyes narrow. "The entire time."

"Uh-huh." I take a step toward the door again.

"Ask her." Maggie gets the indignant look on her face she usually reserves for our parents.

"So what happened?" I cross my arms across my chest, eager to hear her version of the extra practice session with Coach.

She holds up her bandaged hands.

I shrug. "If you're looking for sympathy, you're not going to get it from me. I've got blisters and callouses too. It's part of the game. Shows how hard you've worked."

"She was busting on me for not listening to her, so she made me do serve and smash drills for five hours."

"Which ones?" I do the math in my head.

"Basically, I just had to serve a billion times, and balls were lobbed at me to smash," Maggie complains. "She even made me hit these dumb cones, and I had to stay on the court until I hit fifty of them—twice. Once with my serve and once with my smash. Didn't matter how long it took me." She looks down at her wrapped palms. "That woman is nuts."

I do some quick calculations to figure out that Maggie isn't lying, which reminds me that I have to check a math problem before I go to bed. I'd better do that now. I dash up the steps, satisfied that she's actually telling the truth. Who knew pinky-swears were the way to get my sister to finally act seriously?

"What? No kind words? I just busted my butt on the court for five hours and nothing?" She shouts behind me.

I turn around halfway up the stairs. "You gotta work hard to get good, Maggie."

"Bells," she says, "how can you think it's okay for Coach to make me train like that?" She leans against the railing, looking exhausted.

"You know, Joe always says that if you want to win, you have to work harder than your opponents."

"Exactly." Our dad nods in agreement, having just appeared at the top of the steps. He descends until he's next to me. "And Maggie, this is what Mom and I were talking about when we said you have to be serious about this."

"Serious means that you let a coach torture you for five horrible hours? I actually miss training with Joe now. At least he knows to praise the effort. Coach K only harps on our weaknesses. It's like it's more about her than the players—like our performances reflect only on her."

"Bella is right. If you want to be the best, you have to work harder than the rest," my dad says. "You're lucky that a dedicated coach like Olga Kasinski is willing to take so much time out of her busy schedule to work with you."

"Ha! As far as I'm concerned, the Kasinski way sucks," Maggie says, barging up the steps past Dad and me. "And you're both going to end up riding the crazy train right along with Coach Krazy-Pants if you keep it up!"

My father and I shrug at each other as she passes by, her bag smashing against my shin. As soon as she slams her door shut, I head up behind her to check my math homework. After that it's back to the court. This is no time to take my eye off the ball.

Chapter Seventeen
MAGGIE

"Got it!" Bella yells, well into another home match.

If we win today, our chances improve significantly for playing in the California Classic. It's do or die time. I move out of the way of the yellow ball as Bella backhands it over the net.

Harbor Prep blasts us repeatedly with deep penetrating strokes from the baseline. We need to swing big on both sides, so I run down the ball in the doubles alley and pop a shot over the net.

"Use the correct grip!" Coach K commands from the sidelines.

I freeze and look down at my sore palm wrapped around my racquet. Quickly, I wiggle my hand into the continental grip. I don't get why she's messing with my grip when the ball makes it over the net whether or not I listen to her. But obeying her orders is better than being to subjected to another epic training session tonight. I'll do anything to avoid that torture.

When I look up, the ball is sailing to my side of the court. I pull my racquet back, but I'm too late.

Bella bounds up beside me and murmurs, "What are you doing?"

"Trying to fix my grip," I say, readjusting my hand to the correct position again.

She lets out a deep breath and returns to her spot. "Just concentrate on your game."

"30–30," the Harbor Prep server announces.

Although we managed to take the first set 7–5 after a tough tiebreaker, and we're up a game apiece in this set, Bells and I are a bit out of sync today—we're not rolling over opponents like we normally do. I can think of only one reason why: our coach's constant nagging is causing us to lose our focus.

My thoughts flash back briefly to the tournaments Bella and I played years ago. You know, I never thought I'd miss a person who mostly just told me what to do, but what I wouldn't give now to have Joe on the sidelines instead of Coach K.

Before I set up at the service line, Bella holds up two fingers behind her back, signaling me to poach the net. A second later, Harbor Prep launches a hard serve toward Bella. Bella bounces on the balls of her feet and hits a solid forehand.

Harbor Prep responds with a perfect backhand to Bella's weak side, but I attack the net and catch them off guard. "Got it!" I smack the ball crosscourt, aiming for the outside edge of the doubles alley.

Harbor Prep whacks the ball back to us with another tough backhand.

"Me!" I hit a perfect drop shot that dies once it hits the other side of the net.

Harbor Prep runs it down and attempts to lob the ball over our heads.

I swing the racquet over my head and come down hard on the ball like I've been practicing, excitement coursing through me.

Thwack.

Both Harbor Prep players turn their backs to the ball. It smacks the one standing at the net hard on her thigh.

Oh yeah!

The crowd erupts.

I look over at Coach K for her reaction.

"Don't forget to point with your free hand," she shouts, using her arms to demonstrate the smash from the sideline.

Bella holds up her hand for our handshake. We're doing well enough now that Coach won't blow a gasket over it.

I smack Bella's hand with enthusiasm, but inside I feel queasy. Will my efforts ever be good enough for our beloved coach?

"Ready for my new move?" Bella asks.

"Huh?" I lower my hand, puzzled.

"Come on," she says, hip-checking me.

Since I'm not expecting it, I stumble a bit.

"I added a little hip action to our lucky handshake," she says, grinning. "Think of it as choreography."

"Oh yeah?" I grin and join my sister with some hip-wiggling of my own.

Bella puts her arm around my shoulder and leans in. "Okay, listen up. Both Kristen and Deanna hate the smash," she whispers, pointing to each girl with her racquet. "Keep it up!"

"Let's just win this match and get it over with," I say, exhausted.

"What, so soon? When we're having so much fun?" Bella skips to her spot, her cheeriness impressive, if also a tad grating.

I grip my racquet and refocus on the game, wishing that I could just make Coach K disappear so that I could enjoy it all more fully.

"30–40," the girl Bella identified as Kristen calls out from the other side of the net.

Bella holds up her index finger behind her back. I take a step back, ready to cover the backcourt.

"Match point!" Coach K claps her hands as Harbor Prep's server bounces the ball. "Make sure you come in down the line on those short balls."

Thwack.

Kristen serves another ball our way.

Bella tends to be tentative on these big points, but we need to break their serve to take the match, so I telepathically will her to play tough.

Bella bursts from her spot and takes on the powerful serve. The ball sails back over the net with a wild topspin. It hits our opponent's side of the court and falls flat.

Both Kristen and Deanna attempt to run down the tough bounce, but they're too late. Both girls slam into the net.

"Yes!" Bella holds up her hand to me for another shake. I follow her lead and even add the hip check at the end.

I look over at Coach K in between courts. But her back is to us. I can tell from the tension in her raised shoulders that she's watching Lauren and Minka with her usual intensity.

Bella slaps me on the back. "Nice job, sis," she says. "Both Kristen and Deanna are ranked in the USTA 14s. So this was a big win." Her eyes are bright and she's grinning. Only winning and straight As can make Bella this jubilant.

"Awesome," I say. "Does that mean we're in the California Classic?"

"That's Coach's decision," Bella says. She bites her bottom lip and stares at Coach, who is busy making notes on her clipboard. "It's still gonna be hard for us to break through with Lauren and Minka ranked higher than us. We'll need that wild card spot unless Coach Kasinski lets us play against them."

"No worries." I raise my gaze to the large clock above the stands. Finally, I'll get to have some quality time at the skate park.

We shake hands with our bested opponents, and I walk to the bench to gather my things.

"Nice job!" Sadie says to Bella and me.

"Thanks." I wait for Coach to give us some props too. I look over at her again, but she's still scribbling across her clipboard. I guess I shouldn't be surprised. To her, perfection is expected, not celebrated. No wonder my parents and Bella adore her.

"I'll see you at home, Mags. I'm going to work out at the club for a bit," Bella says to me. "Or do you wanna come?"

I hold up my hands, showing her the worn down bandages. "Time for a break. My blisters are tearing me up today."

"See you at home then," she says. She and Sadie take off across the court, chatting feverishly and giggling as they go.

Cheers ring out and I turn my head to find the source. Lauren and Minka shake hands with Harbor Prep's number one doubles team and make their way over to the bleachers. Lauren shoves in next to me and plops onto the bench. She looks me up and down, her eyes resting pointedly on the gray sweats in my hand. Then she pulls out her phone . . . probably to text her boyfriend or to exult in the fact that no one's going to make her break a nail for the next twenty-four hours. She doesn't seem terribly excited about their victory—in fact she's almost blasé about the win.

A welcome sight distracts me from Disapproving Barbie: Ryan's walking over.

"Hey," I say, happy to see him for so many reasons. I'm pumped to hit the park as soon as possible. I need a major break.

"You ready?" he asks.

"Of course," I say, gingerly peeling off the bandages.

"Awesome match," he says, kissing me on the cheek.

"Thanks." I anxiously pull away and look for Coach, since she warned the entire team about our "extracurricular" activities after already having a one-on-one discussion with me.

"Nice sweats," Lauren says. Minka, who's just joined us, giggles.

"Did you guys win your match?" I ask Lauren.

"Uh. Yeah," they say at the same time, then look at each other like it's an idiotic question.

"Score?" I ask, curtly.

"6–2, 6–0," they say in unison. Then, like robots with identical programming, they simultaneously adjust their long blonde ponytails.

"Oh." I make a face like that's not great news as I pull my sweats over my black skort.

After a few moments, Lauren looks up at me and asks, "Why?"

"Ah. Nothing," I say, satisfied that they played right into my hands. Nitwits.

"What's her deal?" Minka asks Lauren.

"Who knows?" Lauren stands and pulls Minka along to chat with one of the assistant coaches.

I snake my arm through Ryan's. "We'll have their spot. Just give it time," I whisper to Ryan loud enough so Lauren and Minka can hear me.

Lauren casts me a haughty look over her shoulder but doesn't respond.

"No doubt." Ryan nods. "Ready?"

"Yeah. It's been too long." I grab my bag, excited to hit the ramps again.

"Ah, where do you think you're going?" Coach K looms in front of Ryan and me. "You know, you can't actually be an 'Anderson Ace,' despite what the press says, if you haven't actually served an ace."

Ouch. She loves to remind me of any and every shortcoming she might see in me.

"Um, home," I say, momentarily looking at Ryan and letting go of his arm.

"I don't think so," she says.

"I thought that my smash—"

"You might have listened today, but you still have miles to go with your game, young lady." Coach K looks down at her clipboard. I'd love to throw that thing on the ground just like she does when she's extra furious. "You hit fourteen balls with the wrong grip. You foot faulted on three serves. And you forgot to point during two smashes."

"But—" This can't be happening. I look pleadingly at Ryan, who stares at Coach K like he'd rather be face-to-face with a two-headed zombie.

"I thought we already established that hanging out with a boy is not the way you're going to earn the number one spot and make it to the California Classic."

"Wait a second. Are you going to let us play Lauren and Minka for the first spot?" I ask, feeling a surge of excitement.

"I never said that. What I did say is that you are not leaving this court right now. You have practice. Grab the balls and the cones and I'll meet you at court two as soon as I'm done with the *Daily News* reporter."

"But—" I show her my bloodied hands.

"Whiners never win," she says, shaking her head.

I squeeze my eyes shut and inhale sharply in frustration.

"I said now!"

I drop my bag and look at Ryan. "Sorry."

He shrugs. "Maybe later?"

"Yeah." I hang my head. "Right."

I let out a deep breath and jog over to court two as Ryan takes off for the park without me.

Chapter Eighteen

BELLA

On Sunday night, Sadie holds the door for me at Beachwood's state-of-the-art auditorium. Grace told me that it was specifically designed for dance performances, but I still can't help but gaze around in awe. It looks reminiscent of an old-time movie theater, its walls lined with posters of famous shows.

We approach the glass-enclosed ticket counter. The large snack bar to our right is filled with fresh organic popcorn, candies, fruits, and drinks. A long line snakes from its counter past the ticket booth and down the hallway.

"I'm so psyched to finally see Grace perform!" Sadie exclaims. She motions to the attendant for one ticket, waving her B-Dub ID card.

"Me too," I agree, finally not feeling guilty for being away from the courts for an hour. "I can't wait to see the routines." I clap in excitement.

"And how did the tennis champ escape her training routine for the night?" Sadie teases, adjusting her cami. She paired her flowing black dress with slouchy combat boots. "Honestly, I didn't expect to see you tonight."

"Yeah. You and me both," I say, handing the attendant my student badge in exchange for the ticket. "I squeezed in my conditioning this morning."

"Of course that was *you* I saw running the Santa Monica stairs this morning." Sadie tucks a piece of dyed hair behind her ear and looks to me for confirmation.

I smile. "Yeah. That was me: 2,550 steps up and 2,550 down." I spent Friday night tackling my homework and all day today conditioning so I could make it to the recital. This is the final week for me to prove to Coach that Maggie and I deserve a chance to enter the tournament.

"Those stairs are killer," Sadie says, walking toward the auditorium doors with her ticket. "Not that I've ever had to run them. Thank God nobody works me as hard as they do you."

"It's not too bad. I'm a huge fan of the steps. Just look at my calves," I joke, pulling up my pant leg and flexing my calf.

"Did Maggie go with you?" Sadie asks as I shove my ticket stub in the back pocket of my jeans.

"She was at the skate park by the time I got up this morning." I walk into the auditorium and scan the sloped seating for our row.

"She's still riding bikes with the Classic right around the corner?" Sadie asks.

"I'm lucky I can even get her to keep showing up to practice. I'm not going to push it. And anyway, it's not like we're entered."

"Yeah, but you will be!" Sadie exclaims.

"I don't know that yet."

"Didn't Coach talk to you after the match yesterday?"

"No. Why?" My voice rises.

"Well, I don't want to get your hopes up if it's not a done deal, but I overheard Coach the other day after practice talking to one of her assistants, and I think she's going to let you and Maggie play Minka and Lauren tomorrow for the number one doubles slot!" Sadie whisper-screams.

"What?" I nearly yell. My stomach falls faster than a drop shot.

Sadie gestures with her hand to tell me to take it down a notch. "Yup. She said she needs a doubles team to represent Beachwood at the Classic and she doesn't think Minka and Lauren have been playing hard enough—they're more about themselves and their image than the team now. She isn't sure she wants to swap them out yet, but she wants the best doubles pair to represent us. So she said that if you two can beat the best, you're the ones who deserve to be entered."

"Really?" My feet feel glued to the carpet as I visualize myself playing Grand Slams internationally: Europe, Australia . . . What would it feel like to see my name in the international rankings? To meet the professionals on tour? To feel a champion's euphoria, knowing that all my hard work has finally paid off?

Sadie brings me back down to earth. "I mean, given all that, Maggie is taking a huge chance still riding BMX. What if she got injured?"

I shrug. "Sure, I worry about her getting hurt. But I can't stop Maggie. If she sets her mind to do something, I'm powerless. And as far as the other stuff, I'll have to believe it when I hear it from Coach." I pull out my phone to check it just in case Coach is calling me with good news, then quickly text Maggie to remind her about tennis practice tomorrow morning. Coach is holding a double session—an early-morning and after-school practice just like the football team's two-a-days.

"Wait!" Sadie halts, holding out her arms to stop us from proceeding any further down the aisle. "Don't we need to hit the snack bar before we sit down?" She looks over at me.

I shake my head. "No snack bar for me tonight. According to you, I might have the biggest match of my life tomorrow."

"Popcorn will recharge your competitive spirit!" Sadie tries to persuade me.

"Alas, no. Plus, did you see the line?"

"All right, all right." Sadie stops in front of row seven and checks her stub. "This is us." She gestures to our seats.

As I scoot in to sit down, I scan the rows around us to see if I spot any of my old dance friends who, like me, are here as spectators, having given up ballet for other pursuits. But instead of seeing my dance buds, I'm surprised to spot Coach Kasinski three rows behind ours. We make eye contact. I smile and wave at my favorite coach.

I'm so distracted that when I go to sit down, I land partially in Sadie's lap.

"What are you doing, silly?" Sadie says.

"Guess what? Coach is here," I whisper, sliding into my actual seat.

"What is she doing here?" Sadie says a little too loudly.

"I don't know," I say. "Don't you want to wave?"

Sadie leans back and rests her knees on the back of the chair in front of us. "Nah. I'm still thinking about the popcorn."

"Excuse me, ladies," says a voice to our left. We look up to see Coach Kasinski hovering at the end of the row with her arms tightly crossed. The longer I'm on this team, the more familiar that pose is becoming.

Sadie puts her knees down, straightens her spine, and neatly folds her hands in her lap. "Hi, Coach," she squeaks.

"Can I talk to you for a moment, Bella?" Coach points a long finger at me.

Coach observes me as I rise from my seat and carefully make my way toward the end of the row. *This is it. She's going to invite us to play Minka and Lauren tomorrow.* Maggie is wrong: Coach really wants the best for us.

"Yes, Coach," I say in my politest tone, pulling back my shoulders to accept the big news graciously.

"What are you doing here?"

I'm caught off guard by her question and I falter. "I was . . . uh . . . just here to see some friends, since I finished early—"

Coach interrupts me. "I'm not the least bit surprised to see Sadie here wasting time." She rolls her eyes. "But you? I thought you were more dedicated. In fact, I was planning to call you tonight to tell you I think it's time you and Maggie play Lauren and Minka."

A lightning bolt shoots through my stomach. "I really appreciate that, and I'm incredibly excited about the opportunity.'"

"But now I'm questioning that decision because I see you here instead of practicing."

No! I swallow a lump. *Why? Why did I come here?* I knew I should have just stuck to my regular schedule. I thought that—

She keeps speaking before I can finish my thought. "I'm fielding a lot of questions about you and Maggie from the press. There's a ton of buzz about the Anderson Aces."

I gulp.

Coach continues. "But it is a shame you're here tonight. It looks like your sister is rubbing off on you. Bella, you're the one who I thought had drive and dedication. You're someone I could see climbing the ranks as a doubles *and* a singles player. You are the one who is supposed to be a good influence and who could have a bright future of her own." She glances at Sadie. "I thought you were better than this."

"I worked out this morning and I thought that—"

She holds up a silencing finger and makes a show of searching the dim auditorium. "I'm sure you did. But I don't see Lauren and Minka here. Do you?"

I don't bother to look. I know they're not here.

Her roving eyes land on mine. "I don't think that's a coincidence. That's the difference between number one"—she points to the sky— "and number two." Her finger rotates down to point at my chest.

That stings.

"If I was still your age, I would not be wasting my time at some dance recital. I would have been on a court working on my game, especially if I knew I'd be competing with the number-ones the next day."

"You're right," I concede quickly, not bothering to point out I had no idea until just now that we'd be playing Minka and Lauren.

"And I'm going to—" Before I have a chance to explain myself further, she walks away.

The lights lower to total darkness and I wiggle my way back to my seat.

"What did Coach say?" Sadie whispers to me once I squeeze back in.

Before I can answer, the music begins. The spotlights scan the stage and the heavy curtains rise. But I'm too busy texting my dad for a ride home to really notice or enjoy the start of the performance.

When I'm done, I tap Sadie. "I gotta go."

With sad eyes, Sadie mouths, "I figured."

I duck on my way out of the row and dash toward the exit. I imagine Maggie's reaction as I make my way outside. Why did I wave happily like that, thinking Coach would be pleased to see me? Maggie would have seen that tongue-lashing coming from a mile away.

Chapter Nineteen
MAGGIE

"Look who's here!" Ryan hollers when he spots me Sunday night. He rolls his bike up to where I'm standing on the sand bordering the Venice skate park. "Where you been?"

"Tennis." I finish a text to Bella and shut my cell. My hands tremble ever so slightly. Just a few minutes ago, I got a voicemail from Coach K. Tomorrow is our big shot: finally, Bella and I have our chance against the clone duo. Nervousness rolls through my stomach like the waves crashing on the beach beside us.

"And how's that going for you?" Ryan asks, half-patronizing, half-serious.

"It's going," I say. Bells says I have a net game now—a cross between power and poaching. And now it's game enough to take on the best. Minka and Lauren are going down tomorrow morning, especially if I can nail the serve I've been working on.

I rub my hands together like I'm about to devour a meal.

"Ooh, Mags, this is a new side of you. You look hungry enough to consume the competition."

"Oh I am, but today I'm just hungry for some freestyle." I clip my helmet straps together under my chin.

Clunk.

Two skateboarders fly by and perform ollies in unison on the steps.

"Then let's get going!" Ryan exclaims. He and I hurry up the gray ramp to join the rest of the crew. He quickly pecks me before he takes his turn. Then, he drops in fast.

Ryan rides his bike up and down the side of the half pipe, pumping the transition. When he rides up the half pipe again, he reaches the coping, gains air, and throws a barspin, turning his bike and landing perfectly on the concrete with a thud.

"Ryan's getting better and better," a guy with the nickname "Mohawk Mike" and the craziest hair I've ever seen comments next to me.

He's right. "Every time I see him ride, it's like he's picked up five more tricks." I watch as he gains momentum again. The other guys and girls above him on the table stare in awe. "He's definitely fearless."

"We're not the only ones noticing. This guy from a new clothing line showed up at the park the other day and offered Ryan a sponsorship. They said he has the talent and the personality to represent their brand."

"Really?" I remember how it's Ryan's dream to land a sponsorship deal. "I didn't even know . . ."

"Well you've been busy." He pretends to flip his hair.

I laugh along with him even though so much has changed in the past few months. Tennis means so much more to me than it did when I first told the gang at the skate park that I'd be playing. As much as Coach Killer is a drag, tennis is way more now than just a gag to get my parents to take me seriously. It's become something I excel at—something I'm proud of. And when Bella and I play together, it's pretty amazing. After trying out all these other sports and activities over the past couple of years, I realize how lucky I am to have something that just feels right. I'm glad I tried the things I did, but what Bella and I have with tennis is so special that I—

I'm so lost in my thoughts, I almost don't notice Mohawk Mike drop in behind Ryan. He nails a barspin too, but he doesn't come close to the speed or height that Ryan gets with his jumps. Ryan seems to defy gravity—sometimes it's like he's suspended in air.

Our friends await their turn to drop in, all eyes, including mine, trained on Ryan as he rolls up off the ramp next to me.

"There's my girl," he says, planting a sweaty kiss on my cheek as Mike lands another barspin behind him. "You ready to nail some tricks on the pipe today?"

"I'm kind of rusty," I answer, feeling reluctant.

"Aw. Come on. You're a natural." Ryan gives me a light jab in my side.

"It's just nice to be back at the park again," I say. I don't mention that the reason I don't want to try something new is that I don't want to risk an injury the day before my big match.

Mike, who also happens to be in my freshman math class, rolls off the pipe and brakes in front of us. "What? Did the snobs take you hostage?"

"You could say that," I answer, thinking about the extra practices, or should I say torture sessions. I open my mouth to tell them about our match tomorrow morning against Lauren and Minka, but I decide against it. If I keep obsessing over tennis, letting it infiltrate my Sunday fun-day, I might as well change my name to Bella.

"You're up next." Ryan points down at the pipe.

I lean over the side and look down at the steep transition. "Let me warm up on something smaller before I go," I say. I don't want to be like the ever-cautious Bella, but I've worked so hard to get this chance to beat Lauren and Minka. Maybe harder than I've worked for anything. I can't blow that.

Ryan rolls backward. Keeping the bike balanced, he places his feet on the bar. "Come on. Riding is just like . . . riding a bike!" he says slyly. "You never forget."

I can't help but chuckle. "You think you're so funny," I say, pulling my gloves over my blisters.

"You ready to see my no-footed can-can?" Ryan's face lights up.

"Really, Ry? You're ready for that?" I've never seen anyone, except the pros, nail a no-footed can-can.

"You obviously haven't been around recently to witness my latest rad skills." Ryan throws his head back and grins.

"I guess not," I say, rolling down the ramp. I stop at a short ledge to practice my feebles behind the skateboarders. I watch as Ryan waits for his turn on the table, my pegs scraping the concrete as I attempt to balance on the ledge.

A few minutes and a couple of bunny hops later, loud cheers roar from the crowd. I turn around to see what Ryan's up to now.

"He's shredding! Effing awesome!" the guy next to me yells. "If only the sponsors were here now!"

I ride up the ramp on the table to get a closer look at Ryan's latest trick.

It's true. Ryan's blasting bigger than I've ever seen him. He rides from the flat to the transition to the vert back and forth like a pendulum. By now, the entire skate park has stopped to watch him. Ryan must be in his element. He loves it when all eyes are on him on the pipe.

Once Ryan hits the coping on the opposite side of us, he's airborne. He raises his feet from the pedals and spins his bike underneath him. A few people let out gasps like they're watching fireworks. But when Ryan begins to descend and pulls his bike back under him, it hits the coping instead of landing seamlessly on the transition.

I've seen this before with Ryan and he usually comes out okay. But this time, the look on his face says it all. I can't help but turn away, a jolt of fear rushing through my blood.

"Ah, sh—" a girl says next to me.

I have to know if Ryan's okay. I face the ramp and watch in horror as Ryan lets go of the bike and—instead of landing on his knees like he usually does—flies through the air with his hands outstretched and his face frightened. His hands smack the cement; his legs smash against the transition with a loud crunch. A trail of blood follows his limp body as he slides down the pipe. Ryan finally comes to a stop on the flat, his bike on top of him.

Chaos breaks out.

"Ryan!" I scream. Dumping my bike, I sprint down the pipe toward him.

A few onlookers shout, "Call 911!"

When I reach Ryan, he looks up at me, his face creased with pain. "My leg." Blood trickles from his nose.

I grab Ryan's limp hand. I look at his leg, which is twisted underneath his torso.

Mohawk Mike flies down beside us. "Someone get help!" he yells up through the pandemonium.

Ryan squeezes my hand. "It hurts."

I run my fingers across the top of his hand. "You're okay," I lie, willing myself not to look at his mangled leg.

"Is it bad?"

"You'll be okay," I say again as the sirens and my beating heart grow louder in my ears

I grip his hand and turn my head away so Ryan won't see the tear about to slide down my cheek.

Chapter Twenty

BELLA

"Where's Maggie?" Sadie chirps bright and early Monday morning as the team gathers for our match against Lauren and Minka. Now that everybody knows it's happening, there's a definite buzz in the air.

"I don't know," I say, feeling my stomach lurch as I search the courts once again for my no-show sister. I don't get it. We texted strategy a bunch while she was at the park, and she seemed so psyched. All she's talked about lately is getting the chance to match up against Lauren and Minka.

So where is she?

Last night when I arrived home from the recital, Maggie wasn't there. I checked her room again after I hit balls until ten in the backyard, but nothing. And when I woke up this morning, she still was gone. She must have come in later, checked in with our parents when I was already in bed, and then snuck out with Ryan for another late night sesh. I can't believe she picked last night of all nights. She knows how important this match is.

"You don't think she—" Sadie places a delicate hand over her mouth before she goes any further.

But I can tell she was about to say exactly what I've been thinking, what I've been hoping isn't true—that my sister bailed on me, that all her enthusiasm lately has been a complete and total fabrication, that Grace was right and Maggie intentionally set me up for a major disappointment because of some sibling rivalry.

"She's probably just running late," Sadie attempts to reassure me.

It only causes my anxiety level to rise as high as the bleachers.

Sadie continues to try to distract me, but I barely hear a word and continue to look all around me, searching for my sister.

"Where's your twinnie?" Lauren asks in her saccharine tone as she pulls her racquet out of her bag.

"She'll be here," I respond curtly, turning my back toward Lauren and facing Sadie. Even though I don't believe what I'm saying, Lauren doesn't need to know that.

"Hope so!" Minka chimes in. "Wouldn't that suck if she didn't show up?"

I don't react to her sarcasm and walk away. Acting like I just remembered something important I have to take care of, I trot to the locker room to call Maggie, for the fortieth time this morning.

Her voicemail immediately picks up again.

"Maggie, where are you? Why aren't you at school? Call me when you get this." I leave my twentieth message.

I stare at my phone, willing it to ring. When it doesn't, I sit down on a bench and bury my head in my hands.

The door opens, spilling early morning sunshine into the room. I spin around hoping it's Maggie, ready to serve up a lateness excuse. But it's Sadie.

"Is Coach out there yet?" I whisper.

"Not yet." She takes a seat on the bench next to me. "Are you crying?" Her bottom lip juts out and she leans toward me, wrapping an arm around my shoulders and squeezing.

"No," I use the back of my hands to wipe my wet eyes.

"Come on, Bella, she'll show up." Sadie bites her lip.

"We were so close, Sade. If we won today, Coach Kasinski would definitely support our wild card. We would have gone to the Classic and had a real chance. And I—I mean, we . . . would finally . . ." I stop, feeling hot tears push against my eyelids. "I would finally do something. Everything I've done. Everything I've worked for. And now Maggie has to mess it up."

"Maybe something came up?" Sadie tries to console me.

"At seven o'clock in the morning?" I shake my head.

"Do your parents know where she is?"

"I didn't have a chance to ask them this morning, and they're in court now."

Sadie rubs my back. "Well, there could be a good reason. You never know."

"What I know is that she's with Ryan. She left yesterday before breakfast and I haven't seen her since." I let out a deep breath. "She blew off tennis—again!—just like she's blown off everything else in her life. How could I be so stupid?"

"Don't be so hard on yourself," Sadie says. "You couldn't have known."

"But I thought I did know." I look up at my friend. "I was sure that Maggie had it in her. I really thought she changed. Maybe it was just wishful thinking."

"Okay, ladies!" I hear Coach Kasinski's voice boom from outside.

"Are you going to be okay?" Sadie asks as I stand up and shake out my arms and legs.

I take a shaky breath, steeling myself to face Coach and explain that Maggie messed up again. "Yeah. I'll be fine. This is what I wanted in the first place. Right?"

"What is?"

"For her to quit! That's what I wished for when this all started."

I shove my phone into my bag and head out the door before Sadie can respond. She trails behind me.

Back outside, my eyes adjust to the bright sun and coastal fog. We join the small crowd gathering around Coach, who scans the group in a mental roll call.

"Where's Maggie?" she asks, looking at me as if I'm in charge of my twin because we happened to share a uterus for eight and a half months.

"She's on her way," I lie.

Coach sighs heavily and makes a notation on her clipboard. "Well, if she's not here in two minutes, you're forfeiting the match."

Gasps escape from a few girls in the group.

I swallow a lump, but nod, fully expecting the worst.

"Since we don't have a match yet this morning . . . " Coach points to the track beyond the courts. Despite the burnt orange sun in the sky, a thick fog still hovers above the track. "We're going to complete a mile run. If anyone can't make six minutes, we'll do it again."

Low groans ring out.

"Go!" she shouts, and we jog out toward the track.

It's still tough to see in this fog, but I pull my sweatshirt sleeves over my hands and concentrate on the reflection of Sadie's Under Armour running shoes in front of me.

"Oww!" someone screams.

"Lauren!" Minka shouts. "Are you okay?"

Sadie and I stop jogging and squint through the fog. A crowd is forming around Lauren and Minka. Lauren is on the ground, grabbing her hamstring and rocking back and forth. Her face is pinched in pain.

"Someone get ice!" Minka screeches.

"What happened?" Coach pushes through the crowd, arriving at Lauren's side in an instant.

Lauren moans and continues to roll back and forth on the damp grass clutching the back of her thigh.

"I don't know. We were running together and someone tripped her and she fell." Minka gestures frantically.

Tripped? I wonder what Maggie would say about that if she were here. Probably something about how Lauren is just looking to get out of running. Or how her senioritis is so intense that she's realized her boyfriend isn't enough of an excuse; she needs to fake an injury too. But then again, if Maggie were here, we'd be playing already.

"Lauren, what happened?" Coach squats next to her.

"I was tripped!" Lauren wails. "Just like Minka said." She glares at the team. A few girls exchange glances with one another, obviously taken aback.

"We'll deal with the tripping incident later." Coach Kasinski's face is tight. "Right now, you need to focus on what's hurting you. Is it your hamstring?"

Lauren nods between grimaces.

"You!" Coach turns around and points to Sadie. "Get the trainer."

Sadie takes off toward the locker room. I see her pass a figure approaching the back of the crowd. Maggie. Her eyes are swollen—lack of sleep, I assume—and she's still wearing her BMX riding clothes: jeans and a long tee with a brown stain at the bottom. A tennis bag is balanced on her shoulder.

She drops her bag and nervously approaches Coach, who is studying Lauren's pulled muscle. I clench my fists as Maggie comes closer.

"What happened?" she asks.

"Lauren fell," I hear someone in the crowd say.

Maggie scrunches her forehead and takes a few tentative steps toward Coach. "Coach? I'm really sorry I was late. I was—"

"Where is the trainer?" Coach doesn't even acknowledge Maggie.

"I'm sorry, I—"

"Maggie, please." Coach shouts, waving her off. "Can't you see I'm busy?"

"Owwww!" Lauren howls when Coach moves her hand away from the back of her leg.

"But I can explain why I was late. I was at the skate park last night—"

Coach's focus is on Lauren as she responds to Maggie, "Do you not see what's happening?"

"I'm sorry. I just wanted to tell you—"

"I gave you a chance today!" Coach snaps, whirling to face my sister. "And what do you do? Instead of seizing the opportunity you barely deserve, you show up late, looking like you were out partying all night! And then you have the nerve to try excusing yourself by saying you were at a skate park of all things?" Coach's voice drips with disdain. .

"But I wasn't. I was—"

"You just said where you were. You leave me no choice, Maggie Anderson!"

"Wait. I just—"

"Enough! You are done. You're off the team. Go!" Coach points to the locker rooms.

"What?" Maggie's face turns from pale to pink: Her bottom lip quivers. "But—I can explain!" She looks at me to save her.

I cross my arms the same way Coach always does and stare past my sister's plaintive face. I'm not saving her this time, even though she's probably one of the few people here who'd be honest about the extent of Lauren's injuries. Maggie went too far.

Hot tears well at the corners of my eyes. I wipe one away quickly before anyone spots it escaping.

"But—"

"The trainer is on her way," Sadie shouts, jogging up to us. She glances at Maggie.

"Ahhhh!" Lauren yells again.

"Ice." Sadie tosses a bag to Coach, who catches it and places it on Lauren's hamstring.

"It's cold!" Lauren yowls, sitting up and gesturing wildly at everyone. "Get away from me!"

Our teammates start to back away. I spot a few glancing at each other and rolling their eyes. As the group disperses, I catch whispers of "What a faker."

Maggie gets pushed to the side in all the commotion. She hangs her head, watching the girls walk away, then makes her way toward me.

I focus on the blades of grass underneath my running shoes and bite my bottom lip.

Maggie stops in front of me. "I'm so sorry, Bella."

Without looking up, I say through clenched teeth, "We finally had our chance and you blew it."

"I can explain."

"Just explain how you manage to do it." I meet her eyes, anger brimming inside me.

"Manage what?" Maggie's eyes glisten.

"How is it that you always ruin everything?" Another tear escapes and I wipe it before my sister can see.

She swallows loudly. "Bella, I didn't—"

I swiftly turn around and stalk away, leaving my sister to stand by herself.

I spin around after a few dozen steps, ready to give Maggie another piece of my mind, but she's gone.

Chapter Twenty-One
MAGGIE

Coach kicked me off the team, so I figure I may as well blow off school and check on Ryan at the hospital. I bum a ride with a BMX friend, and once I'm there, I find out the deets are even worse than they were this morning—Ryan's fracture is more complex than the doctors initially thought. He needs surgery. We keep him company for the rest of the day, but since there's nothing else we can do for now, I have his aunt drop me off at home later that night.

When I reach the doorstep, my thoughts shift to the other issue occupying my mind: the Classic this Saturday. I yank open the front door, determined to find a way to get back on the team and make this right with Bella. One disaster is enough for now.

It should be an easy fix with Bells, as long as she can get over her initial reaction and let me explain myself. Then I have to make her promise not to tell our parents about Ryan's injury. I don't want either of them getting the wrong impression about BMX—or Ryan.

I'd hate for them to add "dangerous" to their list of three thousand reasons why I shouldn't ride. And the last thing I want is for them to think they have a reason why I shouldn't see my boyfriend.

The moment I'm inside the foyer, my dad is in front of me. His tie is loose and his face is as red as my Red Bull hat. "It's about time."

Behind my dad, seated on the steps with her face buried in her hands, is Bella.

"Thank God you're here," I say, walking toward my sister. "Now, I can finally explain. Want to talk up in my room?"

"Wait, one second, Maggie Lynn." My father steps in front of me. "Leave Bella alone. I think you've caused her enough pain today."

I catch sight of my mother, leaning against the railing and clutching a glass of red wine. "How could you?" she gasps.

"Yes, Maggie. How could you be so irresponsible?" my dad accuses. Veins bulge at his temples.

"What?" I drop my tennis bag by the door. Images of Ryan crashing down the pipe, of the red and blue ambulance lights, and the EMTs putting him on the gurney flash through my mind.

My mother steps forward and places her wine glass on the small table by the door. She points at my stretched-out Vans tee, still stained with Ryan's dried blood. "What happened to your shirt?"

I stare at the blood splotches, thinking of Ryan. My heart twists for him. Even before the accident, Ryan's been in my thoughts way more than any other boy I've hung out with. But if I tell my mom and dad that my boyfriend got hurt riding, they'll take my bike and I'll be banned from the park for good. They'd probably even figure out a way to sue the park for mental anguish or something ridiculous. Worst of all, what if they keep me from seeing Ryan?

"It's paint," I lie.

My mother rolls her eyes.

I look at my sister. "All this drama because I was a little late to practice? Jeesh."

"You think you were 'just a little late'?" Bella screeches from the steps. "You were so late that you almost missed the most important practice of the season. The most important practice of my life!"

"I—"

Bella cuts me off. "So late that you were kicked off the team!"

"But I'm hoping to clear—"

"Hoping what?" my dad chimes in. "That we wouldn't notice when you didn't come home last night? You leave me completely baffled, Maggie. I do not understand how you can continue to act so irresponsibly, dropping activities and friends like trash."

"Don't forget boys," Bella adds.

"I don't drop boys. . . ." I trail off thinking of Ryan.

"Your bad behavior has damaged your sister's chances at success." My mother places her hands on her hips and paces across the hardwood floor like she's in front of a jury. "You should be ashamed of yourself."

"But—"

"Once again, you have selfishly put your own needs in front of everyone else's," my dad continues.

My own needs? Going to the hospital with my injured boyfriend is selfish?

"We should have known you wouldn't take tennis seriously," my mom cuts in. "But we gave you the benefit of the doubt, thinking that was the best decision."

"And instead, we set Bella up for heartbreak." My dad lowers his hands onto Bella's head like a priest performing a blessing.

Heartbreak is watching someone you love in pain.

"I can't figure it out. Was this some kind of ploy to get back at your sister?" My mother glares at me as she swoops by, her heels clacking like horse hooves on the hardwood floor.

"No, that's ridiculous."

"To top it off, Lauren got hurt today," Bella joins in. "We would have been named the number one team without even playing the O'Donnell sisters." Her face is red and splotchy like she's been crying for hours.

My father releases a breath that sounds like steam coming out of a vent.

"You know what? I don't think a simple apology can even come close to atoning for this type of misstep," my mother says. Her lips make a tight line.

"An apology?"

"I agree," my father adds. "Maggie, you're going to have to face serious consequences for this."

"Don't forget school," Bella says, showing me no mercy. "She skipped school today."

"Aren't you going to let me explain, tattletale?" I snap. My throat tightens.

"Do not act like Bella is at fault! Nothing could even begin to explain all of this." My mother stops pacing to pick up her wine glass. She grips the stem with one hand, shuts her eyes, and pinches the bridge of her nose with the other.

How can I explain so they'll understand?

My father smacks his forehead with his palm. "That's right. How could I forget that we received a call today from school? Not only were you kicked off the tennis team, but you didn't attend classes today. Where on earth were you?"

"I . . ."

My mother sits down next to my sister on the steps. She wraps her arm around Bella's shoulders. "Bella told us that a first draft of your picture book was due today. Now Bella's straight As are also in jeopardy because of your bad decisions."

"Do you have anything to say for yourself?" My father positions himself on the other side of my sister. The three of them are like unified soldiers on the frontline of a battlefield.

They'd never listen to me. Their minds are made up.

Once again, I'm alone.

Blood rises from my toes to the top of my head. "You know what I have to say for myself? I have to say that all you guys give a damn about is Bella!"

I turn around, whip open the front door, and slam it behind me. Then I storm down the street and text Ryan's aunt to pick me back up. Even if I have to spend hours in a waiting room, I'd rather be near the one person who truly cares about me than at home with parents who think they only have one daughter worth loving.

Chapter Twenty-Two
BELLA

At practice on Wednesday, I hit another ball over the net to Minka, who barely moves as the whirring blur sails by her. She takes a few lazy steps and picks a different ball off the court.

"Ready?" she drones.

I nod, bouncing on the balls of my feet.

Out of habit, I look to see where Maggie is on the court. And then I remember—no more doubles. Maggie's off the team. The Anderson Aces are over and I'm back to playing varsity singles . . . barely. Minka will be back to playing doubles as soon as Lauren returns, which should be any day now—definitely by the competition this weekend.

I haven't spoken to Maggie in two days, but the word around Beachwood is that Ryan took a rough fall at the skate park and broke his leg. I haven't asked her about it because, one, she's barely been around, and two, I feel like a jerk if that's really what happened.

I still can't think about the Classic without feeling sick to my stomach. I was happy that at least I'd have the chance to practice with Minka today but honestly, so far it's been like playing with a ball machine.

Minka returns the ball to me and I whip a forehand back to her. We play this serve-baseline game, over and over and over again.

"Break?" monotone Minka calls out from the other side of the court after a half hour of hitting. I glance up at the clock to see how much time is left in our practice.

Lauren is sprawled out on the bench near us, sunbathing and occasionally observing our practice. All that remains of her so-called injury is a compression bandage wrapped around her thigh. I head over and grab my water bottle from its spot next to her. Minka rushes over from the other side of the court and roughly wedges herself into the tiny gap between where I'm standing and Lauren is lounging, like her sister is a magnet she can't possibly resist.

"Don't wear yourself out today," Lauren says, pointing her new racquet at Minka. "Big contest this weekend and we're the number one seed."

"Don't worry about me." Minka wipes a bead of sweat from her brow. "Worry about Bella."

Lauren looks my way. "Yeah. Sucks to be Bella."

"Too bad, Bella," Minka says, without an ounce of sympathy.

"How's that injury?" I gesture to Lauren's hamstring.

"Fine," Lauren says. She adjusts her tank. "Thank God it was just a mild sprain." Lauren grins obnoxiously.

"Uh-huh," I say, incredulity obvious in my voice. *A sprain she just happened to get right before we had to run a six-minute mile?* I finish my water and toss the bottle into the recycling bin, thinking about how Maggie had said Lauren was lazy back when she first met her. I wonder what else she's tried to get away with. . . .

Minka cuts in. "You seem a little tense, Bells. I know you hated playing with your sister, but it must really suck to get so close and then end up with nothing!" She twirls her new Penn racquet with a rhinestone-encrusted *M*. It matches the one her sister's been playing with.

I shrug and shove my fingers through the grid of my racquet, adjusting the strings. "What do you guys think of the competition this weekend?" I ask to shift the focus off me.

"Maggie is such a flake. And those Vans and hats? So ridic." Minka wrinkles her nose like something smells.

"Have you heard anything about the other girls playing tomorrow?" I ask again.

"Remember when she wore one sock up and one down?" Lauren interjects. "Loser!"

"Let me know when you're ready," I say to Minka, realizing that having an actual conversation with the O'Donnell sisters is as impossible as winning a match against Venus and Serena.

"I know. And all the boys she hangs around with? They must like her *for some reason*, if you get my drift." Minka nudges her sister.

"Yeah. I heard that Tommy guy *really* misses her."

"I'm sure he really misses what Maggie gave him."

That's enough. "You know what I miss?" I ask, channeling my sister's spunk.

"What?" Lauren asks. "Your tennis career before your sister decided to pick up a racquet and ruin it?"

"Oh my God! That's a good one." Minka laughs.

"No. I really miss when you and Minka didn't talk to me. Remember? When you didn't think I was worth it? That's what I miss. Because you two are a couple of idiots." I spin the butt of my racquet between my palms like a whirligig the way Maggie used to during practice.

I can't believe I ever thought Minka and Lauren were all that. They might be good tennis players, but they're awful people.

Maggie has her faults, but at least she's not a diva. And after playing with Minka the robot today, I realize Maggie was right: We could've beaten the crap out of these two. Too bad my sister messed this up before we had the chance. Maggie's heart has always been three times bigger than her head, which is part of why she's such a good tennis player. But it gets her into trouble. It would be just like her to show up late for the most important match of her life because she was comforting an injured Ryan.

Lauren narrows her eyes at me in contempt.

"Whatever." Minka shrugs and drifts to the court with a scowl.

I thought I'd be happy to be back by myself on the courts, but it just doesn't feel the same. With Maggie, I was better. With Maggie and her grunts, spins, and energy, tennis was more fun. With Maggie, I had a chance to finally do something big. And now I'm back to just plain old Bella. And it stinks.

I do know one thing for sure. I have to try to fix this before it's too late.

I wait by Coach's office after we finish the conditioning drills that wrap up our practice. She's powwowing with the assistant coaches, and when they leave, I rub the sweat off my palms and tap underneath the gold nameplate on her door.

"Come on in," her voice bellows from inside.

Walking into her office, I'm immediately taken aback by the enormity of her impressive collection of championship trophies. What I would do to have an assemblage like Coach Kasinski's.

Coach looks up from her desk. "Hi, Bella. Nice job out there today." She takes off her bifocals and sets them next to a pile of books.

"Thanks," I say, standing at attention in front of her massive desk. I take a deep breath and clasp my hands tightly behind my back.

"Have a seat." She points to two leather chairs. "What's on your mind?"

"I actually wanted to talk to you about Maggie," I say, carefully lowering myself onto the chair.

Coach's relaxed expression instantly becomes tense. She leans forward over her desk once again and grabs a pen from the mug. "Go ahead." She taps the pen rapidly against her opposite palm.

"It's recently been brought to my attention why Maggie was late to practice last Monday. It was a situation that was grossly out of her control. She was actually helping a friend who was injured. And I was wondering . . ." I clear my throat. "If there was any chance she could be reinstated to the team." I stare at my hands folded on my lap.

"Absolutely not." Coach says without hesitation. She uncaps the pen and begins scribbling on a sheet of paper.

"Even if the reason for her lateness was warranted?" My voice quivers. A trickle of sweat rolls down my back.

Coach tosses her pen on her desk and sits up. "It's very nice of you to stick up for your sister, but it must be exhausting for you to defend her every time she makes a bad decision."

I pick at the hem of my skort.

"Look, Bella." Coach lets out a deep breath. "Believe it or not, I was in your tennis shoes once upon a time." She turns a picture on her desk to face me. It's a photo of two girls, about eight or nine, who look identical. They are smiling, gripping tennis racquets with their arms around each other. "I have a twin, just like you."

"You do?"

"Yes. And we played doubles together just like you and your sister. That's why I took such an interest when I saw the two of you play together at the club this summer."

I stare at the picture and figure Coach and her sister must've won tons of trophies. But I don't remember hearing anything about her sister.

"I keep this photo on my desk to remind myself of something. Like Maggie, my sister had enormous talent. And like you and your sister, we were set to take the tennis world by storm. But then when we were teenagers, my sister gave up on tennis, and my coach, my parents, everyone just let her quit. Just like that. Done."

Coach turns the photo back to face her again.

"In retrospect, I'm kicking myself for ever thinking your sister could be different. I was wrong about her. And so are you. Maggie is just like my sister: a quitter." Coach shakes her head. "Quitters never win."

"But she didn't quit," I squeak. "You kicked her off the team."

"She behaves like a quitter. I haven't heard from Maggie since the day of her expulsion." She pauses. "I don't understand why you're even here. If Maggie hasn't taken the time to explain her actions, then why should you?"

"She hasn't?" I ask, wondering why not.

"No," Coach says. Her icy blue eyes send shivers down my back. "And if Maggie wants back on the team, it should be her who's having this conversation with me, not you."

I sit up straighter. *So there's still a chance.*

"Let me give you some advice—from someone who's been there. Move on. I know I have."

I bite my bottom lip to keep it from quivering. I know Maggie doesn't want to quit. She never would have attended all the extra sessions and trained with me if she didn't care about tennis. In the end, I think she may have been into tennis even as much as she's into BMX. But if Ryan was hurt as badly as everyone says, of course Maggie would go with him. She'd never leave a friend who needed her, especially not Ryan.

I feel a deep pang of regret that I never let my sister explain herself to me. I thought she was being selfish showing up late like that, when in actuality it was the opposite.

"Anything else you'd like to discuss?" Coach asks, picking up her pen and tapping it impatiently against the page.

"No. Thanks for your time," I squeak. I turn around and shuffle out of Coach's office.

I can't just let Maggie walk away. We have to make this right.

Chapter Twenty-Three
MAGGIE

I stare into the bowl at the skate park Wednesday afternoon, ocean waves crashing behind me. We couldn't have asked for a better day in Venice. The wind is light, the sky is clear, and the ocean glistens as seagulls cry in the distance. Too bad I can't enjoy it.

All I can see when I look into the bowl is the blood pooling next to Ryan as he lies still on the flat. I hear the sound of his leg snapping in half and smell the alcohol and IV fluids as the paramedics put him on a gurney and roll him into the awaiting ambulance. It's all too much. . . .

"You okay?" Mohawk Mike asks, stopping behind me so suddenly that it causes me to jump.

"No. I mean, yeah," I say, balancing on the table on my Mongoose. How can I possibly drop in the bowl again after everything I witnessed?

"The first day back after watching someone wipe out is always the hardest," a girl who always lands a wicked can-can says. "How's our man doing?"

"Better," I say. I stopped to see Ryan at his house this morning before school. "He's got a cast now."

"He was so lucky, dude," Mike says.

I flash back to the injury, the blood, and the ER. "He is lucky," I murmur, pulling my bike back from the coping. "I think I might just stay on the steps today." I roll my bike toward the ramp to the mini. "I'm really not feeling the half-pipe."

"Yeah, I'm with you on that one." The girl rolls behind me. "At least you have tennis to keep you busy, right?"

I look over my shoulder. "Not exactly."

"Why? What happened?"

"Same thing that happened before," I say without elaborating. "I should have known better."

After I complete a few grinds, I'm surprised to spot Bella standing on the graffiti-covered barricade by the park entrance. Palm trees sway above her as she scans the area. I sigh and attempt another ice pick on a step, stalling on a back peg while the front of the bike is off the ground. What is *she* doing *here*? She spots me and heads in my direction. I ignore her and focus on my bike.

"Can I talk to you for a sec, Mags?" she asks once she reaches me. She looks suspiciously at Mike, who is balancing on a step nearby, like she thinks he's a spy or something.

Just a few days ago, I was the one pleading with Bella to listen to me. But she wouldn't. Instead she formed an anti-Maggie alliance with our parents. Why should I talk to her when she wouldn't give me the time of day?

"Shove it," I say, riding across a mini ramp and completing a bunny hop.

"Come on, Mags. Look, I didn't know Ryan was hurt," Bella yells out.

"You would have if you'd listened. But you just assumed the worst of me."

Bella's shoulders slump and she looks defeated. "I know. I'm sorry."

"You have two seconds." I brake in front of Bella. Over her shoulder, I catch one of our friends nailing a double peg grind.

"Way to go!" I cheer, ignoring the family drama for a minute. We need the cheers after Ryan's injury.

The girl from earlier gives me a thumbs-up after landing one of her famous can-cans.

"You need to talk to Coach. You have to apologize so you can get back on the team."

I fiddle with my gloves, pushing them further down on my fingers. "I don't need to do anything."

Bella deflates. "I thought you cared about tennis. I thought you wanted to win big. What about—"

"I did, but it's not worth it. Everyone just judges me. You, Coach K, our parents—all of you think I'm just an irresponsible loser." I grip my handlebars. "So forget it. I don't want to play tennis when everyone involved hates me."

"No one hates you!" Bella exclaims, standing in front of me so I can't ride.

"You wouldn't even hear me out. You wouldn't let me tell you that the only reason I wasn't home Sunday night and was late to practice and missed school is that I was at the hospital with Ryan. Everyone just assumed I was off partying or something."

"I told you, Maggie, I'm sorry." Bella juts out her lip. "The only reason everyone reacts that way is because of your history."

I roll my eyes. "See? You'll never get it." I roll my bike forward until I'm centimeters from Bella's ballet flats. "Are we done? I'd really like to get back to riding."

"Is he okay?"

"Who?" I snap.

"Ryan." Bella's eyes glimmer in the sun.

"Like you care."

"I do," Bella says.

"All you ever say about Ryan is that I'm seconds away from replacing him."

"Is he okay?" Bella presses.

"He'll be fine," I snap.

"How fine?"

"He has a nasty compound fracture." I grimace for a moment, remembering.

Bella brings her hand to her mouth.

I disregard the look on my sister's face and concentrate on the ocean.

She reaches for me. "It must have been so scary. And to think that all of us from tennis were listening to Lauren the faker complain about her hamstring when Ryan was dealing with a real injury." She looks at me even more intensely. "Did it happen here?"

I nod and stare at the gray concrete. "You didn't come here to talk about Ryan," I tell her. "You came to talk about the thing you actually care about: tennis. Why on earth should I put myself through that whole thing again? When you, Coach K, and Mom and Dad are going to torture me about it? For the gazillionth time."

"That's not true." Bella crosses her arms. "It didn't have to go this way, Maggie. If you had just called to tell me about Ryan right after it happened, all of this could have been avoided. I left you, like, a hundred messages that morning, and you didn't even bother to text me back."

"Calling you wasn't exactly the first thing on my mind," I say, unhooking my helmet. I remove it and hang it by the straps on my handlebar.

Bella stares into my eyes. Her chest inflates slowly and I can tell she's feeling sorry for me. "This must be really hard for you."

I don't want her sympathy. I don't need anyone to feel sorry for me. I just want to be left alone. "I like playing tennis, but it isn't the world to me like it is to you. There are other things in my life that are just as important—or more. So can you please get out of my way so I can ride?"

"It's not just about tennis, Mags. It's about doing the right thing, being responsible, taking accountability. I understand why you didn't call me, but if you had we wouldn't be in this mess."

"You want to talk to me about doing the right thing?" I feel my eyes well up. "I *did* the right thing. I was there for my boyfriend. And then I tried my best to get to that damn practice for my sister."

A tear rolls down Bella's cheek. "I know that."

Seeing my sister cry always wreaks havoc on my emotions. I need to get back to riding before I lose control. I adjust my messy ponytail, pick up my helmet, and shove it on my head. "Please, just go," I say, snapping my helmet straps together. "I can't go through this again. This is just like when we were eleven and everyone gave up on me."

Bella sniffles. "No one gave up on you, Maggie."

"Yeah, they did. Mom and Dad completely turned on me."

Bella wipes her eyes. "They wouldn't do that, Maggie," she tries to reason.

"Yes, they would. They did. They waited until I screwed up, then left to watch you—the perfect child."

"Watch me? What are you talking about?"

"Why do you think I flipped out and fired that ball that hit Joe?"

"What?" Bella's glistening eyes widen.

"That's right. I quit the first time because I was tired of it. Tired of always being the loser." My voice quivers. "I can't believe I set myself up again."

Bella lets out a shaky breath and uses her sleeves to dab her eyes. "Maggie, I apologize for not listening to you. But I didn't know any of this. I didn't know how you were feeling. I wish you had said all of this earlier because I would have told you that no one thinks you're a loser," she says, clearing her throat. "It's the opposite."

Tears are dangerously close to escaping my eyes. I hate crying. I never cry.

"Can't we just figure something out? We were so close to really making our mark. If you made it back on the team, we might even be able to do something huge this weekend. We're so close."

"Bella, it's over." I stare at my front tire treads. I don't want to be reminded of how amazing we were on the courts. It was like magic. Now it's gone. And that hurts.

"No, Mags. It's not over. Think about it. If we could win this weekend, we'll qualify for all the big tournaments." She pauses. "Can you imagine?"

"Once again, all Bella can think of is points and rankings." I roll my eyes, then dab them gently with the back of my sleeves. "Look, I just want to practice my grinds, okay? Can you get out of my way?" I want Bella to leave so I can ride my bike and forget about all this heavy stuff. The past couple days have been tough enough without all this garbage.

"The Classic is Saturday. We might still have a chance."

"And?" I push my bike forward. Bella steps back when I'm an inch from running over her feet.

"I went to see Coach today about getting you reinstated on the team."

"You did what?!"

"Just hear me out okay?"

I rest my feet on my pegs and cross my arms.

"Coach said that if you wanted back on the team, you would have to talk to her yourself."

"Fat chance," I snap back. "I'm never talking to that—"

"We're good together, Mags." Bella stares deep into my eyes imploringly. "Our tennis is something special."

"Bells . . . it's really—" A knot wraps around my stomach and I can't finish my sentence. She's right. Our tennis is something special. When Bella and I played together, I had more fun than I ever have.

"Just think about it, okay?" Bella asks. She grabs my hand and gives it a quick squeeze. "Please."

Chapter Twenty-Four

BELLA

My hands tremble as I clutch the half-finished picture book in our creative writing classroom Thursday morning. I feel like I'm going to vomit.

"What is that?" Lauren stops in front of my desk before class starts. She points at my book and curls her lip in disdain.

I stare down at my perfectly crafted words surrounded by blank paper. The cover is half gritty and half sparkly to show off the different personalities of the twins, just like Maggie and I planned. But that kind of unity is a lie. The book is still missing its second half: the illustrations.

"OMG." Lauren's frame casts a shadow over me. She holds out her finished picture book. A Maggie-type thought occurs to me, and I find myself wondering who she paid to do the project for her. "I guess Maggie couldn't stop at just ruining tennis for you, huh?"

I sigh and keep quiet. I've got nothing to say in response, and in a way it feels like she's right.

"My partner and I managed to get ours done, and we're both injured." She snorts.

Injured. Yeah, right. Coach still won't let Lauren play, but I don't buy that anything's wrong with her hamstring at this point. Ryan on the other hand . . .

"You know," Lauren continues in a rare moment of biting perceptiveness, "Ryan isn't a bad partner. He's no Brandon Teisch, but I can see what your sister sees in him."

I remain silent, not letting myself get into a verbal skirmish with my teammate just before we have to present our projects.

"Guess she did one thing right, huh?" Lauren taunts, smirking. "But I figure that doesn't make up for what she's done to you, now does it?"

"Okay, class. Let's get started," Mr. Ludwig announces from the front of the room. Lauren takes the cue to get to her seat.

Maggie isn't even here, of course.

I shove the book underneath my notebook, embarrassed by the incomplete assignment. I put my chin in my hand and dejectedly picture the F on my report card. I thought that maybe, just maybe, stubborn Maggie would finally come around after all my pleading at the skate park. But once again, I was dead wrong. I don't know why I even bother.

Mr. Ludwig glances at me. "Since Maggie isn't here yet, Lauren, you're up first." She leaps up and bounces toward the front of the room.

I sink further into my seat.

The classroom door swings open and Maggie shuffles in. "Sorry I'm late," she mouths to Mr. Ludwig. He nods back at her. Everyone at Beachwood seems to be cutting Maggie some slack after hearing she's been helping Ryan, or at least everyone besides Coach Kasinski.

I stare at her Element book bag like I have X-ray vision. Even though I know it's a long shot, I can't help but hope the illustrations are inside.

"Hey," she says to me, without any indication that she notices I'm practically having a panic attack. "Where's the book?" She holds out her hand.

I pull it out from underneath my notebook and hand it to her.

"Great." She snatches it up and by the time Lauren is done reading about a frog and a princess (a story that sounds suspiciously unoriginal) and sharing Ryan's cartoon-like illustrations (which look suspiciously like something my sister would draw), Maggie's done plastering sheets of paper into our book.

"Bella and Maggie, you're up!" Ludwig announces.

I inhale sharply, wishing I wasn't here. Maggie's been either at the skate park or at the hospital. There's no way she had enough time to draw suitable illustrations for both books.

Maggie's eyes are wide with excitement. "Ready?" she asks me, springing out of her seat.

Here goes nothing. I nod. I probably should be used to Maggie embarrassing me by now.

I trudge to the front of the room and offer a tentative smile to Mr. Ludwig, hoping he'll take it easy on me, and more specifically my grade, after he sees this book. Maybe I can talk to him after class about getting me some extra credit so I'm not held back by my sister's attentions being elsewhere..

"Our book is titled *Different Strokes*," Maggie begins. "The theme of the book is tolerance."

Okay, so maybe she did put forth a little effort?

Maggie hands the book over to me. Of course.

"*Different Strokes*, written by Bella Anderson and illustrated by Maggie Anderson," I say, cringing as I open the cover. At least Ludwig knows that I wrote it and I'm not responsible for the drawings.

I take a deep breath and look down at the page before me. Scanning the illustrations, I'm astonished. The first page is a flawless watercolor of a little girl in a pink tutu holding a racquet. This one alone must have taken Maggie hours to complete. I hold the book out so everyone can get a look. When I make eye contact with Mr. Ludwig, he looks pleased and nods his head.

I begin to read. "Bianca loves ballet, but she also loves tennis." I turn the page and take in an adorable illustration of a girl in bike gear holding a tennis racquet. I show it to the class. "Madeline loves tennis, but she also loves biking. Together, they are quite a pair. But one day, Madeline gets angry at Bianca and quits tennis."

I continue reading and proudly displaying my sister's work. The illustrations are exquisite. I glance at Maggie, who stands next to me brimming with delight.

"Even though Madeline madly loves biking, she misses playing with her sister. Secretly, Madeline begins practicing tennis again." I continue to page through the story. A close-up shows each girl wearing one tennis shoe in the foreground. In the background, it's just possible to make out the other shoes on each of the girl's feet: Bianca wears a ballet slipper while Madeline wears a hightop sneaker. "When Bianca and Madeline put their best foot forward, they become champions. After tennis, Bianca dances and Madeline rides her bike. It is double the fun for this pair of aces." I shut the book and beam.

The class bursts into cheers. Sadie even whistles. Mr. Ludwig stands up, calling for an ovation, which makes Maggie blush.

"That has to be one of the best books I've seen since I began assigning this project ten years ago," Mr. Ludwig tells us approvingly. "Wonderful theme, illustrations, and creative writing. Together, you two *are* a pair of aces."

Maggie and I look at each other and smile. Then my sister grabs my hand and we take a little stage bow.

Chapter Twenty-Five
MAGGIE

After Bella and I ace our picture book, I leave to have lunch with Ryan.

I reach his cozy canyon house a few miles from Beachwood and lean my bike against a thin tree before sprinting up the steps to knock on the front door of the two-bedroom Craftsman-style house. A pumpkin rests on each side of the concrete front steps.

"Come in," I hear his mom yell from the back room.

I push open the solid oak door and step onto the polished hardwood floor. To the left in the tiny living room, Ryan is spread out on the leather couch watching coverage of last year's X Games. A thin striped blanket is pulled over his legs and a scented candle flickers on the TV stand.

Ryan leans his head backward and his face lights up. "Hey, babe!" he says and moves the blanket off his lap. His casted leg rests on a pillow.

"Don't move," I say, rushing to his side. Even though the doctors told Ryan's mom that his recovery has been quicker than normal, I still like to make sure he's super careful.

"I'm fine," he says, grimacing as he gingerly repositions the blanket. Two blue and white hospital bands are still wrapped around his wrist.

I dig into my pocket and toss a bag of Now and Laters on the table beside him.

He points the remote toward the TV and hits pause. "Thanks, dude," he says, dropping the remote and reaching for a piece of candy.

Before he can get there, I open up the pack for him.

"How's the leg?" I ask.

"All good," he says, popping a Now and Later into his mouth. Fading yellow bruises still cover his eyes and part of his nose.

"You still look like you went ten rounds," I say, staring at the gash under his eye that hasn't healed.

"Yeah. I know."

"Here, honey." Ryan's mom walks into the living room. She hands Ryan his pain pills. He takes them with his good hand and tosses them into his mouth.

"Thanks, Mom," he says, washing down the medicine with a cup of water she gives him.

"Sure thing, hon." She looks at me and smiles gently. Her eyes are the same pretty blue as Ryan's. It's clear he inherited them from her. "Maggie, you've been such a huge help through all this. We can't thank you enough." Her bright blonde hair frames her heart-shaped face.

I stare at my black Vans. "It's no big deal," I say, feeling my cheeks heat up.

"Every morning and every afternoon, you come to keep Ryan's spirits up, bringing his favorite treats and picking up the slack when I can't be here."

"It's all good," I say, smiling at Ryan.

"You're such a sweetie." Ryan's mom rubs my shoulder. Her strong perfume tingles my nose. She lets go of my shoulder and grabs her keys and oversized Marc Jacobs handbag. "I'm going to run an errand. I'll see you crazy kids later."

A second later the door shuts behind her.

"What are you watching?" I ask Ryan, even though I already know the answer. I fall in the brown lounge chair across from him and rest my feet on his couch.

"The X Games, of course," he says, starting the TV again. "Watch this!" He scrolls through the footage and points at the TV as last year's gold medalist rolls up the pipe and completes a no-footed can-can.

I cringe when I see the trick again.

"Now that's how you land it," he says, pointing at the television.

"How can you watch this?" I ask, feeling like the Now and Later I just ate is stuck in the back of my throat.

"What do you mean?" He turns down the volume on the TV.

"How can you watch the same trick that put you in the hospital without even blinking?"

"How can I not?" He shrugs.

"Because . . ." I decide not to say that I've been struggling lately.

I'm struggling with the fact that I don't know if I could handle getting injured at the park. It could mess up so much for me.

"I have to see where I made my mistake." He looks at me like I'm crazy. "The doctor said I can ride again in about six months, as soon as this stupid leg heals. Look at this double backflip," he says, pointing at the television as Dave Mirra, the winningest X Games rider, completes the trick. "Completely badass."

I feel the familiar sink in my stomach as I wait for Mirra to wipe out like Ryan did. He doesn't. Instead, he lands safely on the other side of the quarter.

"So you're really serious about getting back on your bike as soon as you can?" I ask. Ryan attempts to sit up straighter and pain flashes across his face.

I rush to his side and adjust the pillows behind him.

"Thanks." He looks into my eyes and smiles. "And yeah. I can't wait to get back out there. Sitting around this place is making me crazy."

"Aren't you worried it's going to happen again?" I ask, staying by his side on the couch in case he needs me again. "And what if the next time—"

"Nah." Ryan shakes his head before I can go any further. "Broken bones and injuries are part of the sport. You can wipe out, learn from it, and then get right back on the bike. It's like staring death in the face and spitting at it every time you drop in on a vert."

I ponder his words. I respect his courage, but I don't know if I have the urge to look death in the face. I hate to admit it, but I'd rather stare down a tennis opponent.

"Enough about me and this stupid wipeout." He smirks. "What about you? How's the park? What jumps have you been nailing?"

How do I tell him I haven't set foot on the pipe since his injury?

"I haven't really had any time to ride lately." I pick at the seams of his striped sheet.

"That's not because of me, is it?" he asks. "You didn't have to do those book illustrations. . . ."

"Nah," I say, and continue to trace my finger along the stripe. "Actually, I haven't exactly been able to get on the pipe again since . . ."

"My accident?" Ryan holds out his hand toward mine.

I grasp it.

I stare at my hand intertwined with Ryan's. His middle finger rests across mine, the knuckle where he broke it last year attempting a barspin. I take a deep breath. "Tennis," I finally say.

"Tennis?"

With any of the other guys I've hung out with, I'd have already delivered my "I think we're better as friends" speech by now. But I don't want to run away from Ryan—I want to run to him. Could that be because I'm no longer running from the one thing I'd been avoiding this whole time—tennis?

The sun shining through the curtains turns Ryan's cobalt eyes a bright blue.

I squeeze his hand, willing myself to explain. "I feel like, in a way, your injury showed me that tennis means more to me than I thought."

"Huh?"

"Like, this whole time I've been missing something."

"What do you mean, you're missing something?" Ryan's eyes squint as he attempts to understand what I'm saying.

"This whole time I've been going from sport to sport and activity to activity and really all along, I've been avoiding what I really care about—tennis and everything it represents . . . my sister, my parents, my former life."

"You don't care about riding?"

"Oh, I still love BMX." A bead of sweat rolls down my back. I guess I'm not used to being honest with boys.

"But—"

"I quit tennis a few years ago because I was hurt. It wasn't the sport that hurt me—it was my family. I lost my temper and quit something that meant a lot more to me than I thought." I look up. "And all this time I've been trying to find something else that captures how I used to feel when I was playing tennis with Bells. Your wipeout scared the crap out of me—not because I don't want to ride, but because I don't want to get hurt and lose tennis again. Because I guess tennis is basically like my true love." I finally spit it out.

"What?" Ryan's eyes are the size of a bike tire. "I thought you were kicked off the team. I thought you never wanted to swing a racquet again!"

"I was and I didn't. But both times I quit, it wasn't really because I hated tennis. I hated the way my family made me feel. Instead of dealing with it, I quit. And pretty soon I hated myself for quitting. Then I looked for something to take its place and . . ." I stammer. "And someone to take my family's place."

"So what changed? Why are you now realizing all this?"

"It was the book."

"The book?"

"Today in creative writing, Bella and I rocked our project. Ludwig said it was the best picture book he's ever seen. It just got me thinking that Bella and I could do something really great together with tennis too."

Ryan smirks.

"What?" I say playfully, and very gently poke him in the stomach.

"Aw, man! You're giving in." Ryan falls back on his pillow dramatically.

"Hey!" I tap his shoulder lightly.

"I knew you were going to buy into the whole organized sports thing."

"Come on, don't you know me better than that?" I poke him again. "But I'm serious. You know how you're pretty much a natural at tricks and when you're on the vert, it's easy for you? And even if you get hurt, you want to go back out there and ride again? You're fearless and all that."

Ryan lowers the arm he'd draped across his forehead to block the sun from his eyes.

"That's kind of how I am with tennis. It comes pretty easy to me, and now that I've gotten past my initial anxiety over being back, I don't have a hard time with the pressure," I say, sitting up a little straighter. "I'm fearless on the court."

"So you're going to give up riding?" His eyes look so sad I can tell he's thinking that BMX isn't the only thing I'm about to bail on.

"I'm not giving up anything." I squeeze his hand reassuringly. "I'm adding something." I smile. "I'm going to really give tennis a shot—you know, give it my all right now."

"But what about *Coach K*?" He says her name with disdain. "I thought you hated her. I thought she kicked you off the team."

"I set up a meeting with her after school today."

"And you're sure you want this?"

I nod. "I've never been so sure of anything . . . except, you know, us." I lean in for a kiss, placing my lips against his so that there's no confusion about my meaning. Our lips part ever so slightly as he gingerly sits up, and I feel his strong hand begin to move up my back. I'm breathless as we hit our rhythm and I don't want to leave. Ever. But then I remember my meeting. I pull away. "You don't think I'm punking out, do you?" I say, out of breath.

"Nah." Ryan shakes his head, beaming (though I'm guessing it's not about my participation in tennis). "You're not. Because it's still on your terms."

"Exactly," I say, winking at Ryan.

"That's my girl," he says, opening up his arms.

I fall into his chest, carefully.

"You know what I thought while I was laid up in the hospital?"

"What?" I lift my head so we're eye to eye.

"That I'm pretty lucky to have my own Maria Sharapova."

"Sharapova, and a rider at that."

Ryan gently kisses me and we lie with my head on his chest, watching the X Games highlights. Once his mother gets home, I jump on my bike and bolt back to Beachwood to face the music . . . and Coach K.

Chapter Twenty-Six
BELLA

Joe pulls his Prius into a parking space at the UCLA Tennis Center for the big tournament on Saturday morning. I'm glad to have him back. So much has happened while he was gone.

Of course, the comfort of his presence doesn't really make up for his dragging me to the first round of the California Classic. "Can you explain to me again why you're making me come to this stupid tournament?" I whine. Obviously, I think the Classic is anything but dumb, but it's hard to be positive when Coach Kasinski refused to register Maggie and me. She'd told us, "You always have next year." At least she let my sister back on the team, but she wouldn't agree to more than that.

Joe smiles underneath his Nike tennis hat. "I just think it'll be good for you to check out the competition."

"And be tortured."

"You did bring your gear, right?" Joe ignores my dramatic

remark. "We have a lot of work to do this afternoon. I've been away too long. So plan on being at the club with me until at least seven."

"Of course." I roll my eyes. "My gear is in your trunk."

I sigh loudly, thinking about how Joe deserted me for clinics this last month as I climb out of his car and walk the lush grounds of the campus toward the facility. I've practiced at UCLA occasionally, but the tennis complex always takes my breath away. It's a lot like Beachwood's new facilities, only bigger. Joe and I make our way past Pauley Pavilion to the courts. We enter at the top of the outdoor stadium, and below us, three blue courts line up symmetrically. On the side, a white-tented area awaits the players, and I allow myself to daydream of lounging there before a match.

Joe and I begin our descent to our bleacher seats, passing tons of girls clad in various tennis gear, surrounded by coaches, pros, and parents. This is it. All the best junior tennis players are here to take part in the Classic. It's the top thirty-two teams and sixty-four kids in California. I gaze longingly at the gorgeous courts, desperate for an opportunity to play. But there's no chance for that now. "This stinks," I say, shuffling behind Joe toward our spot.

"There's my winning attitude," he teases. "Hey, look at today as an hors d'oeuvre."

"An hors d'oeuvre?"

"It should make you hungry for more."

"Believe me, I'm starving. I've been hungry for my shot for a long time." We pass two girls I recognize from tournament play. They're about to begin practicing on court three. Both are ranked higher than me. If only Maggie and I had a chance to play them, we might change that.

We reach our seats and get settled. "How much you want to bet you'll be playing here soon?" Joe holds out his hand for me to shake it.

"Not as a doubles player." I shake his hand.

Joe leans back on the bleacher behind us and stretches out his legs. "Stranger things have happened," he says.

"Bella!" A shout rises from the court below.

I look around nervously, expecting to see someone else I know ready to rub my face in the fact that I'm a spectator instead of a player today.

"Bells!" the voice calls out.

Joe nudges me and points to my sister, Maggie.

She's standing mid-court, holding a racquet in one hand, dressed in a black tennis skort and powder blue tank. "What are you doing up there?" she shouts.

"Huh?" I shrug, looking at Joe, who smiles mischievously.

"Get down here! We gotta warm up." She bounces on the court, causing her chocolate ponytail to sway. From a distance, with her tan, lean frame and her outfit, she actually looks like she belongs down there with the rest of the participants.

"What?" I shout, shaking my head to see if that will help her words register.

"We're playing today!" she yells again.

I gasp and look to Joe again. "Told you you'd be out there!" he says. He thumps me on the back. "Go talk to your sister."

I charge down the bleachers. I grab Maggie's arm and pull her to the side of the court. "Is this some sort of sick joke? Because you're embarrassing me in front of—"

"No. I'm totally serious." She smiles, catching the irony of that statement.

"But wait." My mind runs over yesterday. "How could this be? Coach Kasinski said she wouldn't enter us."

"Joe didn't tell you? I called him because I knew he'd just gotten back. He ended up talking to the tournament director and found out that there was a last minute scratch. So he gave them a recommendation and worked with me to convince Coach K that she shouldn't stand in our way."

I shake my head, still trying to make sense of all this. "What?"

"Yeah, he called me last night to let me know we were entered."

"He got us in?" I look up at Joe. He waves and smiles.

"Yup." She beams back at him, her expression turning mischievous. "And well, I guess *I* did too."

I open my mouth to say something more, but I've got nothing.

"You better get your skort on. We're scheduled to play our first match in an hour."

I bounce around a bit like Maggie was doing earlier. But then the reality of what she's saying hits me. "Mags, please, you have to promise that you'll stick with tennis this time. Because . . ." I shake my head. "I can't bear to lose all this again."

"Don't be such a stiff." Maggie playfully hits me on the behind with her racquet. "And get dressed. I need somebody to practice with."

I giggle, thinking about how times have changed, then turn around and sprint up the bleachers. "I can't believe you let me wallow in my misery like that!" I exclaim as soon as I reach Joe's side.

"Eh, it would have been too easy to just let you think you were in." Joe tosses me the keys. "Where's the fun in that?"

"What if I'd been so sad that I just gave up tennis entirely?"

"Bella," he says, placing a hand on my shoulder. "I've known you a long time. You would have been fine."

I skip to the parking lot to grab my bag from his trunk.

Chapter Twenty-Seven
MAGGIE

For our second match, Bella and I were set to play two of the top singles players from Santa Barbara, who paired up for the tournament. It's been an uphill battle since the match began. Bella wasn't kidding when she said the Classic was tough.

"Come on, Mags," Bella says after I miss another smash. "That's the fifth time today."

"Game," the official calls out. "Three games"—he points to our opponents—"to five games." The chair umpire points to us.

As we switch sides, I see Coach K mouthing, "Technique! Technique!" and demonstrating the correct grip with a pretend racquet. Apparently, she insisted on being present even though she had almost nothing to do with us being entered.

Bella steps up next to me on our way to the other side. She whispers, "I've played Sing Yi and Tory before.

I glance at the opposition and take note of their pink tennis dresses, pink headbands, and matching pink hair ties. Both girls look like they take their clothing advice from Malibu Barbie.

"They like to hit drop shots as much as they like the color pink. Be ready for them."

"I'm sure she has some advice." I point to Coach K.

"Don't worry about Coach." Bella hugs her racquet and glances at the sideline.

"You know she's back in our corner now because she wants to take credit for us."

"Just worry about the match." Bella walks to her spot on the court.

With the set score one all, Bella and I are tied for the first time since we began the varsity season. In the first round, we managed to win two break points in the first set and then bring several others to deuce. In the end, my left-handed forehand and Bella's penetrating groundstrokes were too much to overcome.

We might have won the opening round 6–4, 6–2, but Bella was right. This tournament is tough, and we're not going to roll through these matches like we do during the regular season. Our goal is to make it at least through to the elite eight if not the final four or the championship.

Sing Yi bounces the ball before tossing it into the air. She shouts, serving it hard my way. Reacting on instinct, I forehand it back over the net. "Hee!" I grunt.

"Low to high!" Coach K instructs, which ignites a fire in the pit of my stomach. Who does she think she is waltzing in here and coaching us?

Tory hits a drop shot, her sequined hair tie glimmering in

the sun. Instead of charging after it, I watch as the ball falls over the net.

"Mags!" my sister shouts.

"15–love," the chair umpire calls out.

"Concentrate, for God's sake!" Coach K continues to berate me from the sideline. I hang my head and walk back to my spot at mid-court.

I look over at Joe, who points to his temple then claps and gently says, "You got this."

Bella rocks back and forth on the balls of her feet. She signals one finger behind her back, signaling me to poach the net. "Just play your game."

Sing Yi bounces the ball twice again. I squat down in my ready position like Bella, preparing to explode. Sing Yi winds up her racquet and grunts as she fires the ball our way. Bella returns it with a blistering forehand. I'm anticipating the short drop shot return. Instead, Tory hits it deep.

"Got it!" Bella backhands the ball over the net from the baseline.

Tory poaches the return and hits another drop shot. But because Bella told me what to expect, I'm ready for it this time. I run down the ball.

Sing Yi hits a shallow forehand my way.

"Got it," I shout. I look up and spot an opening between Tory and Sing Yi. Without stopping to think about my technique, I backhand it hard, right on the money. The ball skips in between both girls, flying past them.

"Way to finish!" Bella stops for our handshake on her way to the back of the court.

"15–all," the chair umpire announces as we hip-check.

I can't help but smile. I turn around and wipe the sweat off my forehead before it drips into my eyes. From the stands I hear, "Go, Anderson Aces!" I look up to see my mom and dad seated together clapping. They're even holding up a sign. For a moment, I flash back to my last tournament—my parents leaving, Joe, his nose.

I shake it off, but the distraction makes me miss Bella's sign. I squat in my ready position as Sing Yi tosses the ball in the air once again for the serve.

The ball screams between Bella and me.

I momentarily space out and the ball bounces between us just like the shot I nailed a minute ago.

"30–15."

Bella places a hand on her hip. "Mags!"

"What?" I shrug.

"Urgh."

"Let's not start," I say, bouncing on the balls of my feet again.

"Pay attention," Coach K shouts at me. "That was ridiculous."

Joe holds two fingers up to remind us to work together.

I look down and wander back to my spot then turn my head toward Bella, who's still staring at Coach K. For a second, I swear she narrows her eyes at Coach.

Bella is glaring at her idol? No way.

I don't have time to dwell as Sing Yi once again tosses the ball in the air and serves. Her serve is so fast Bella doesn't have time to react. The ball bounces hard and ricochets crosscourt. Bella doesn't get to it. And I stand like my feet are glued to the court, still stymied by Bella's recent turn of behavior. Bella stares at the ground and mumbles to herself.

"Ace!" the chair umpire calls out. "40–15. Game point."

I shrug it off and find my spot again. I focus on Bella, who holds up two fingers behind her back.

A few seconds later, another Sing Yi serve screams toward us. Bella steps out of the way and I return the ball with my backhand. The ball smacks against Bella's thigh.

"Urgh!" Bella shouts.

"Maggie!" Coach K chastises from the sideline. "Get out of her way!"

"Game," the official says.

Bella and I jog off the court, heads low, for a water break. Coach K is waiting for us at the white bench.

"I told you, Maggie, if you didn't listen to me, I'd take you off the team for good," she shouts, pointing in my face. "Do you think that was a joke? You are on thin ice, so you better start paying attention. Do you hear me?"

I hate this woman.

I look away from her bulging eyes and anger-flushed face and focus on the blue court instead, reminding myself that it's about tennis, not Coach K, not my parents. I'm here to play tennis because I love the game and I'm good at it. If I talk smack to Coach K, I might hurt our chances to do what we've set out to do.

"And you, Bella, I don't know what has gotten into you." She yells even louder this time. "You need to play your game out there!"

Bella takes a deep breath.

"You are embarrassing me, your school, and our program." Her voice rises a decibel with each word. "This is exactly why I didn't want the two of you here in the first place."

"It's just—"

"Don't say a word." Coach points in Bella's face, her long finger centimeters from Bella's nose. "I don't want to hear your whining and your complaining and I especially don't want to hear any excuses. Just go out there and play the Kasinski way!"

Coach Kasinkrazy storms away.

Bella tosses her towel on the bench.

"Don't listen to her," I say, leaning my racquet on the bench. "She's not even our coach today."

"We've just got to get in sync again." Bella studies her water bottle before taking a sip.

Joe approaches us. His Nike hat casts a shadow over his brown eyes. "Is everything all right?" he asks.

"It's just Coach K," I say. "She's—"

Bella cuts me off. "It's fine, Joe. We're just out of sync this match."

"Spend some time and regroup. Then take a deep breath and play this match like it's any other. You both have nothing to lose today. Remember that." Joe pats us both on the back and returns to his spot on the sidelines.

"This game is ours. I can feel it," I say.

"Oh yeah?"

"Yeah. Because the good side always wins."

Bella tips a water bottle to her mouth.

"Just think about what Joe said. Because *that*"—I point at Coach K, who is furiously scribbling on her clipboard—"is definitely not good."

Chapter Twenty-Eight
BELLA

As I'm drying off my tank with a towel, my eyes wander to the tented players' area. My eyes settle on someone whose stare is directed our way: Lauren. She's playing today for the first time since her "injury." She glares at us with a satisfied smirk on her face, like she just loves watching Coach Kasinski scream at us every few seconds.

I glance back at Coach, muttering to herself on the bench. And then my eyes dart to Joe, who's clapping and giving us a thumbs-up. Lastly, I check on my parents, who just look nervous.

Maggie pours water over her head. She shakes it off, flinging water droplets all over me.

"Mags!" I shout as the cool spray hits my skin.

She points her racquet at me. "It's time to kick some butt."

I chuckle as I finish my water. Maggie always manages to be like a sunbeam after a foggy morning.

"This is not the time to clown around!" Coach K—oops, Kasinski—shouts.

Maggie freezes.

But I don't. Something has been slowly dawning on me. All this time, I wanted to believe that Coach Kasinski was the best tennis coach on earth. She's not. She's a decent coach surrounded by great players. Maggie is right. She's in it for herself. She's in it for the glory. She's out to prove something that she couldn't prove during her own playing career. She uses her players to make herself look good.

For the first time, I get what Maggie meant when she said, "Who cares what Coach thinks as long as we're having fun?" Maggie was right not to place stock in her. I forced Maggie to change, to play by Coach Kasinski's rules, so I could get what I want. That makes me almost as bad as Coach. I can't do that anymore.

So today, I make up my mind. Instead of my usual petrified apologies, I stare right at Coach Kasinski and pour the rest of the water over my head and shake it out playfully.

Coach slams down her clipboard in disgust.

"Yes!" Maggie cheers, grinning wider. She breaks out in our victory dance.

"Let's do this, Mags," I say. "You and me."

We jog to the other side of the court. The ball girl tosses me a tennis ball and I walk behind the baseline. *Bring it on.*

I signal to my sister. "Ehh!" I shout as I serve the ball powerfully to Tory, our opponent in pink. Tory's glorious forehand spins the ball my way. But it doesn't faze me.

Is that all you got, Tory? This is an elimination tournament. I thought you would bring more than that.

I easily move behind the ball and backhand it to her partner, Sing Yi, who gets under the ball and slices it over the net. If I know Sing Yi, after a slice she'll be flat footed. "Mine!" I attack the net and drop a shot far from Sing Yi's reach.

Sing Yi stretches for it, but her feet anchor her to the court. Tory attempts to run it down, but she's too late.

Gotcha.

Clapping erupts. I hear my dad's signature whistle from the crowd as Maggie and I complete our handshake.

"Use your slice," Coach Kasinski demands from the sideline. "You're better than that. Show the other team your skills."

More like show the world our skills so Coach can take credit for them. I can't believe I didn't see it before. Maggie was right: it's never been about us.

"15–love," the official calls.

Maggie and I slap hands. "Let's do this," I say, signaling a two. Maggie nods, bouncing at mid-court. I toss the ball into the air and hit the serve.

Sing Yi backhands the ball to me. I respond with a deep forehand. The topspin causes the ball to die on Tory and Sing Yi's side. Sing Yi gets to it and hits a hard backhand to Maggie.

"Hee!" Maggie magically gets to the ball and backhands it with an insane angle.

Sing Yi charges the net and hits the ball before it bounces. It takes an awkward spin toward Maggie who runs it down and backhands a high blooper to Tory. *Not good.* Tory has an amazing smash. Tory whips her racquet and—sure enough—hits a perfect smash to Maggie.

Instead of turning her back to the ball like most players do in reaction to Tory's power, Maggie holds out her racquet. The ball pops off the racquet and skims the top of the net. It falls over on Tory and Sing Yi's side. Tory and Sing Yi stare in shock.

"30–love," the official announces.

Coach Kasinski claps her hands swiftly. "Play smart tennis! You could have used your forehand."

"It was in, right?" Maggie says to me as we slap hands and hip-check. "Because the way Coach K is flipping out, you would think I hit a ball out of play."

"Must be that crazy train she's on." I snicker, using Maggie's term.

"Think for once, Maggie," Coach Kasinski shouts and jabs a finger against her temple. "Play smart or you'll be making up for this with extra practice."

I roll my eyes at Coach and look over at Joe. He points to his bicep—a signal to remind me to focus on my strengths. Once again, I find my spot behind the baseline. I catch another toss from the ball girl. Then I wind my racquet and nail it. The ball slams between Sing Yi and her partner, Tory. Neither one moves.

"Ace. 40–love," the chair umpire announces. "Match point."

"Terrible technique!" Coach Kasinski yells from the sidelines.

Joe whistles and my parents politely clap. I see them whisper to each other and I wonder if they're discussing my technique.

Maggie slaps my hand. "Nice one!" she says, ignoring Coach. "You put the ace in the Anderson Aces."

"Thanks, Mags." I lean in close and channel Joe. "Don't listen to her. Just play your game and focus on your strengths. You're awesome."

Maggie winks and then swings her hips dramatically.

I can't help but let out a cackle. And I don't even hold my hand in front of my mouth to hide it from Coach Kasinski. I signal to my sister and toss the ball into the air again. I whip my racquet and nail it. The serve sails over the net.

Sing Yi hits a backhand my way.

"Ehh!" I grunt, returning her backhand with one of my own.

"Mine!" Tory shouts sprinting down the ball. She pops a high one behind me.

But I can feel that Maggie's there. She eyes the ball and whips her racquet for the smash. "Hee!" she shouts.

Sing Yi turns her back to the shot as it bounces in front of her.

"Match," the chair umpire announces.

Maggie runs up behind me and jumps on my back. "That was my best smash ever!"

"We held them to love. Maggie, you're killing—" But, before I can finish my thought, Coach Kasinski is in front of us with her arms crossed, of course, and her face tight with rage.

"You may have just won, but that was terrible tennis!" she screams.

Maggie lets go of my back and charges toward the bench past Coach, muttering, "Whatever."

I inhale sharply and walk past her too.

"What did you just say to me, Maggie Anderson? Both of you get back here this instant! I'm not done talking to you!" she screams after us. "You better fix that sloppy play you call tennis, or—"

"Or what?" my mom calls from the side of the court. I turn to see her and Dad walking toward us.

I freeze because I can't believe my eyes. And from the look on Maggie's face, she can't either.

"What are you going to do about it?" Mom and Dad stand now on either side of Coach Kasinski.

"Hello, Mr. and Mrs. Anderson. It's so nice to see you on this gorgeous Saturday afternoon. Congratulations on the win today. It looks like Maggie and Bella are moving on to the next round. You must be so proud. I've worked very hard with both Bella and Maggie to get them to this level."

Mom and Dad exchange puzzled looks.

"We are very proud of our girls. However, we've been listening to the way you speak to Maggie and Bella," Dad begins, "and—"

"Your verbal threats straddle the line of battery, Ms. Kasinski," Mom says in her filibuster voice.

"Humiliation and intimidation certainly are not effective when it comes to our daughters," Dad adds. "And I can't imagine those less than stellar communication techniques foster tennis achievement in any of your charges."

Coach Kasinski looks taken aback for a moment, but soon recovers. She smiles like a Cheshire cat. "That's interesting. I would think you'd have more respect than to insinuate that my technique is inappropriate. Are you aware of my background, Mr. and Mrs. Anderson? I'm one of Beachwood's most celebrated coaches. Time and time again, I've demonstrated that my techniques *do* work."

Joe joins us, congratulating Maggie and me on the win. He

glances to my parents then back at me as if to ask, "What's going on?" I smile then look pointedly in my parents' direction.

"Your past achievements have no bearing on what we're discussing right now, Ms. Kasinski. Past success or not, you're out of line with your harshness," Mom says.

"Your insults are not only demeaning to our daughters, they constitute verbal abuse." Dad is not messing around.

"And we will not tolerate it." Mom has his back.

Coach does not retreat. "I disagree. My coaching methods have been proven effective for twenty-five years."

"That doesn't make them acceptable and it certainly doesn't mean they will work for our daughters," Mom says.

"Maybe your daughters just need to toughen up," Coach Kasinski volleys. Big mistake, judging by the looks on our parents' faces.

I step back and watch in admiration, and partial embarrassment, as my parents call out the coach on her nasty ways. I'm surprised to find I don't even need to deep breathe. I don't feel anxious.

Maggie and I head to the bench to relax and enjoy the show. "This is the best seat in the house," Maggie whispers. "Coach has no clue what she's doing, going toe-to-toe with them. Mom and Dad never lose arguments."

"I know," I whisper back. "This is it for Coach Kasinski and us." I say, feeling a bit more trepidation suddenly. *Without Coach, what will I do? Where will we play tennis? Will we be off the team at Beachwood?*

"Your daughters wouldn't even be close to where they are today without me," Coach Kasinski challenges my parents. "And without me, they won't go further."

"Are you're threatening us?" Dad asks.

"Just stating the facts," Coach answers. "You should be aware that your daughters will never get to the top without me."

"Wanna bet?" Maggie can't help but insert herself into the conversation.

Coach Kasinski throws up her arms. "I'm done with this conversation, and I'm done with the two of you."

"No!" A cry escapes my mouth. This can't be happening.

"I have no intentions of coddling your daughters—they've already had quite enough of that from the looks of it. And I have no interest in coaching children whose parents don't understand the value of tough talk and exacting standards." Coach stomps away, leaving my parents, Joe, Maggie, and me on the sideline.

"What just happened?" I ask frantically, watching my tennis career implode in front of my eyes. "I need—"

"Don't worry about it," Dad says. "You're not going to work with that woman anymore."

"That's right." Joe steps in. "Let's focus on the moment. You two are unstoppable today. Your communication is phenomenal and so is your court coverage. Excellent work. I can't tell you how excited I am to watch you girls play again."

But Joe's comforting words can't calm me right now. The anxiety I'd been surprised wasn't plaguing me earlier rears its ugly head. I take slow, measured breaths and start to recite what I know. "Coach Kasinski holds the golden key to tennis superstardom. She's coached more champions than—"

"So?" Maggie wraps her arm around my shoulders, sensing my distress.

"Girls, I'm so sorry that we didn't realize sooner what a monster Coach Kasinski is." Mom walks over and squeezes both of us for a second. Hugging isn't really her style. She's more of a tap us on the head and tell us she's proud of us every once in a while type of mom. But this situation merits a brief hug, apparently.

"She's not—" I stop myself, still deep-breathing. I swallow a lump. "My entire tennis career rests on this match. What if we lose? What then?"

"Aw, come on, Bells! We've made it this far," Maggie says.

"Yes. You girls are on fire," Dad says in his gruff voice.

"The buzz I'm hearing in the bleachers is the Anderson Aces are the newest sensation. I wouldn't let a little tussle with Ms. Kasinski get in your way," my mom says. "You don't need her."

"Yes, I do." I attempt to swallow again, but I can't because my mouth is drier than the court.

"Anyone want something to eat?" My dad changes the subject. "I'm starved."

How can they eat at a time like this?

"Me too! And I'm thrilled that we're done with that witch. Now we can have some real fun." Maggie smacks me on the butt with her racquet. "Let's go, tennis twin! Our next match is in two hours. I'm hungry for some nachos and I heard the Student Union serves up some good grub." She skips toward the cafeteria.

I look at Joe, my head heavy. "What am I going to do?"

He shrugs. "Get some nachos with your sister and focus on the next match. We'll deal with the other stuff later."

"Nachos aren't an option right now."

"Why's that?" asks Joe.

"Because I think I'm going to throw up." I burp, then throw my hand over my mouth in embarrassment.

Joe taps my back, like he does when I lose a match at a tournament. "Everything's fine, Bella," he says. "It will work out."

Unfortunately, I don't believe him.

Chapter Twenty-Nine
MAGGIE

"Want some?" I ask Bella, who is too busy sulking to enjoy the mouth-watering Cheez Whizzy nachos the Student Union serves.

"No, thanks." Bella sighs.

Back in the stands, we watch a tight semifinal singles match. Coach K shouts instructions from the sideline. I snicker.

"What are you laughing at?" Bella asks in a monotone. "What could possibly be funny when the best high school tennis coach just blacklisted us?"

"Good riddance!" I say, finally at ease now that I don't have to worry about Coach K screaming in my face every ten seconds.

"What's in those nachos? Because you must be hallucinating."

"Do you know how many tennis stars get discovered playing high school tennis?" I ask my sister.

"Of course I know. None. But how would you know that?" She eyes me suspiciously.

"I know a thing or two!" I inform her. "All that time you thought I was messing around, I was mostly reading tennis websites. When I was at the hospital and helping out Ryan, I'd read while he slept. And when I got home and everyone was asleep, I'd practice on our court. I'd alternate between drawing the picture book and practicing tennis."

"You would?"

"Uh-huh. I dig it! Tennis, that is. Though the painting and drawing was fun too."

"So you really are serious about tennis? You're not gonna bail on me to try something else?" She twists to face me.

"No way. I was just *trying* out other stuff. But now I know: tennis is what I really love." I down another nacho and wait until I'm mostly done crunching to continue. "It's what I'm best at and I like that we get to spend time together. Now if I could just change the super girly, stiff outfits and wear something more normal than this"—I pull at her skort—"then the sport would be perfect."

"Knowing you, you'll find a way," Bella says. She smiles and I hope she's starting to worry less about what happened with Coach K.

"You think? Maybe I will!" I look slyly at her. "But you're the one who's really going to do something one day and make your mark. You're so dedicated."

"I might be dedicated, but you live your own life and do things your own way, even with Mom and Dad always chiming in with their opinions. I don't think I could do that. You're fearless."

"You think I'm fearless?" I recall how shaken up I've been since Ryan's injury. "It's not that cut-and-dry." I dig a chip into the cheese.

"You try out everything—sports, boys."

"Ha!" A nacho falls out of my mouth. "I don't try out boys."

"What would you call it?"

"It's more about experiencing what life has to offer. The boys are just a bonus." I shove another nacho in my mouth. "I told you: it's like a buffet."

"So what's the deal with Ryan?"

A sparkle shoots through my stomach at the sound of his name. "What do you mean?"

"This is the longest any boy has been around."

I shrug and lick imitation cheese from my finger. "I guess he's like tennis—I like him the best."

My sister grins and hits me on the shoulder. "Aw . . ."

"Stop it." I hit her playfully back.

"I wish I'd find time to do different things too. You know, I never wanted to give up dance," Bella blurts out. She places her hand in front of her mouth like she always does when she says something she shouldn't have.

As if I hadn't already been sensing this for, like, ever. I drop the chip I'm holding into the cup of cheese. "I'm actually not too surprised. I kind of always knew you missed it. *I am your twin, you know*."

Bella slowly lowers her hand. "The only reason I quit was because I thought I had to dedicate everything to tennis if I wanted to get here. And I know Mom and Dad wanted me to."

"But you do want to be here, don't you?" I ask her. I place the nachos on the bench beside me and wrap my arm around my sister.

"I do. But I'm tired of my life being so stringently planned out all the time."

I give her a squeeze. "I hear that. I'm claustrophobic just think-ing about your daily schedule."

"I do want to play tennis, but I want to do it on my own terms like you do. I don't want to have to feel like tennis is my entire exis-tence. I'd really like to join the dance group again *and* play team ten-nis." She pauses. "I think . . . I think that I need to stop caring about the rankings and start concentrating on what makes me happy."

"And what's that?" I ask, on the edge of my seat.

Bella scrunches her nose, a guilty expression on her face. Then she blurts it out: "Playing at a level that isn't all consuming."

"That makes a lot of sense to me," I say, thinking about how I plan on hitting the skate park with Ryan tonight after the tourna-ment. "Do you still want to play today? Because if you don't want to, I totally understand."

"Of course," Bella snips. "I have to."

"You don't have to. You don't have to do anything you don't want to."

She puts her hands to her head and massages her temples.

"But it would be pretty awesome if you did. If you played today the way you want to, and if you did *both* the things you love in the future. Heck, if *we* both did both. I'll ride and play tennis and you can dance and play tennis. And we'll kick butt on the court to show Coach K and everyone else that we're badass. We can play the way that works for us."

"That's what I want," she says, looking at me.

"The doubles final, featuring the Andersons against the O'Donnells, will begin in twenty minutes on Center Court," the loudspeaker booms.

"Wait. Did they just say we're playing Lauren and Minka?" Bella's eyes practically double in size.

I rub my hands together like I'm savoring the moment, then raise my arms in victory. "Yes! Finally!"

Bella smiles and shakes her head. "I can't believe we're playing the O'Donnell sisters! I've been so busy with all this drama, I didn't even think to check the bracket. We're not prepared. We need to discuss a strategy!"

"Let's just do it!" I shout. "Let's win this match. Let's play *our* way—on our own terms!"

Bella considers for a moment and then smiles at me. "That's right. The Anderson Aces are taking the tennis world by storm!"

"We're Anderson Amazons," I say, holding up my hand for a high five.

Bella slaps it. "Let's go warm up. You heard the announcement. We only have twenty minutes."

"Wait one sec," I say, grabbing the plastic container. "I have to finish these nachos. No way I'm letting a single one go to waste!"

"You can't eat nachos before a big match," Bella whines.

"Watch me." I shove a cheese-covered chip into my mouth.

"All right, all right. Maybe it does work." Bella takes a chip and digs it into the cheese. "I'm in."

"Always helps my game!" I hold out the container toward her and Bella grabs another.

Chapter Thirty
BELLA

Lauren prepares to serve in the doubles final. This is it. Whoever wins this set wins the Classic. So far, we're even at one set apiece. We almost went down last game, but a lucky ace erased the match point and evened this set at 5–5.

We can't lose now. Bottom line, we have to win by two games.

Lauren tosses the ball into the air and comes down hard with her racquet, her blonde ponytail swinging. I move to where I anticipate the shot will land, but the ball hits the tape.

"Fault," the official calls.

"Yes!" I pump my fist as Lauren glares at me.

Without Coach K (I've decided to call her that too since I know how much she loves it) barking orders at us, the court is quieter than a library. I walked by her in the stands earlier and overheard her bragging about how the doubles final is all her girls. She's been clapping for Lauren and Minka, but doesn't say much to us. Her face is tighter than the strings in my racquet, probably from keeping all the criticism bottled up inside.

Lauren serves again, and I take a deep breath. The ball rockets toward Maggie. She steps aside as it hits just outside the box.

"Love–15," the official calls out.

"Come on, Lauren!" Minka shouts, placing her hands on her hips.

"Whatever." Lauren waves her off. She bends over and touches her toes. "Worry about your own game."

"Believe me, I do worry about my game, and I actually work for it, unlike you." Minka rolls her eyes.

I smirk as Maggie and I do a quick hand slap.

"There you go, girls. Now capitalize like I know you can!" Joe calls from the sideline.

"Yeah. We should keep making them talk to each other so they bicker," I say to Maggie. "Plus, it's obvious Lauren is gassing, so let's take advantage of her weak side."

"Yeah. Maybe she shouldn't have faked that injury. She obviously needed the practice."

"Right?" I agree.

The ball girl tosses another bright yellow ball to Lauren as she moves to the other side of the court. I signal to Maggie and we adjust accordingly. Lauren bounces the ball then tosses it into the air.

Thwack.

She smacks the ball to my side.

"Hee!" I practically do a split to return it with my backhand.

Lauren forehands the ball. A short shot skids toward me.

I hold up my racquet. Before I make contact, I survey the court then pop the ball shallow to the deuce alley slot Lauren always leaves open. Lauren attempts to sprint to my shot, but she tanks.

It drops untouched.

Minka throws down her racquet in disgust. "You're such a slacker and you're killing me!"

"Shut up!" Lauren fires back. She stretches out her hamstring, no doubt looking for sympathy or an excuse.

"Give it up. Your leg is fine."

"Love–30," the official announces.

I turn around to face a smiling Maggie and we slap hands and bump hips. "Told you the nachos are lucky," Maggie says.

I roll my eyes. "I just hope the nachos don't make an appearance on this court. This match is tight and my stomach is a mess right now."

Tap. Tap. Lauren bounces the ball twice. She tosses it in the air and hits a hard serve down the *T* between Maggie and me.

"Got it!" Maggie says behind me.

When it's returned, I know I can poach the ball. I step in front of Maggie. "Mine!" I shout and she intuitively covers the backcourt for me. I slice the ball right over the net.

Lauren and Minka crash into each other attempting to retrieve the ball. Minka manages to get a piece of it but it sails past the white baseline behind us. "Damn it!" Minka curses, pushing her sister as she rises to her feet.

"Out. Love–40," the chair umpire says. "Game point."

"Good call," Joe shouts to us. "Way to work together."

"Exactly what I was thinking," Maggie says, tapping me in the butt with her racquet.

"Come on, Lauren! Get it together," Minka yells. Lauren ignores her sister as she tosses the ball high and smacks it our way. I return it hard to Minka. Minka hits a quick backhand. The ball lands in front of me again, so I follow through and it sails over the net.

Thwack.

Another backhand to Maggie. Maggie returns the ball and Lauren's eyes widen as she spots an opening to my right. I anticipate it and step to my right to get a good jump. My racquet meets the ball, and it trickles over the net.

But Minka is the (comparatively) smart one. She stretches out and gets to it. Again.

We rally back and forth four more times until Minka sees that Bella and I are both at the net. She attempts to poke the ball behind us. Again, I predict the shot and sprint back like I'm about to catch a football deep in the zone. I raise my racquet and point at the ball with my other hand. Then I wind up and smash the ball over the net with everything I've got.

Lauren decides to save herself so she can finish the match in one piece. She turns away from my shot and it bounces high in front of her.

"Game!" the chair umpire announces.

The stands erupt in cheers as we break their serve and are up a game. Lauren turns away from a yelling Minka as Maggie and I do our victory routine.

"If we can hold our serve, the championship is ours," I say to my sister. "Come on, Anderson Ace!" I smack her with my racquet.

The smile slides off Maggie's face. She takes a deep breath and makes her way to the line. The ball girl tosses her a ball to serve. Maggie misses it and it rolls behind her. She gives me a look I haven't seen since she had to get her tonsils out. "I wish you could be the one to serve."

Chapter Thirty-One
MAGGIE

A few minutes later, we're tied again, 15–all. And the only reason Lauren and Minka have fifteen is because I double faulted. I need to focus. This is no time for unforced errors.

The ball girl tosses a brand new Penn my way. I catch it, breathe deep, and bounce the ball twice off the back of my hand then once on the ground for good luck. I have to do this.

I toss the ball into the air and hit it with everything I've got. It soars past Minka.

"Out!" the official shouts.

I hear giggles from the players' area and the stands, and swear I hear someone whisper, "I can't believe she made it this far." Hot tears threaten the corners of my vision.

"Deep breath, Maggie." I hear Joe on the sidelines.

Once more, I bounce the fuzzy ball off the back of my hand and on the court. Then, I toss the ball into the air and whip back my racquet. "Hee!"

The ball torpedoes over the net. It hits the ground in front of Minka and she slams it back my way. "Got it!" I shout as I forehand the ball back to the other side. Minka hits the ball to Bella who backhands it. Lauren's eyes enlarge. She hits an ugly blooper deep.

"Hee!" I hit another forehand. Minka follows my shot, assuming the ball is out.

It hits white.

"In!" the official yells. "30–15."

Minka tosses her racquet on the court. "This is bull! That ball was out!"

More cheers ring out, louder this time. Lauren argues with the official over the call.

While the clones are quarreling, Bella and I complete our handshake and hip dance. "Keep forcing them out of the game they like to play. That's where they break down."

"You're right," I say. I can do this.

Tap. Tap. I bounce the ball twice on the back of my hand and once on the ground, then toss the ball into the air and bring my racquet to the backscratcher position. I extend my arm and reach, keeping my chin up.

Thwack.

The ball drives over the net.

I exhale in relief. I served another one.

Lauren returns the serve to my left.

"Hee!" I forehand the ball awkwardly over the net.

Minka rushes the net, sending a sharp volley to Bella. But Bella tricks her. Instead of volleying it back, she uses her best shot, the two-handed backhand, and spins a sharp ball over the net.

Minka has no chance. It ricochets off her arm.

"Minka!" Lauren shouts. "What was that?"

"Shut up, slacker!"

"40–15," the official announces. "Match point."

Bella jumps a bit, pumps her fist, and jogs over to me for our handshake. "Let's put 'em away!" she says as we hip-check and the crowd cheers louder, anticipating the win.

I stand behind the baseline as the ball girl tosses a ball my way.

This is it.

My heart pumps hard. I'm breathing fast. I can't feel my fingers. My inner voice begins battling itself.

Come on. You can do this.

No I can't. Bella is the real tennis player.

This is your sport too. Go for it!

I toss the ball into the air. "Hee!"

Lauren steps quickly to the side as the ball lands just beyond the service box.

"Out!"

She pumps her fist. Minka walks over to slap hands. I hear her say, "We got them."

Warm tears of frustration well once again.

Then Bella's in my face, calming me down. "Come on. One more. Don't do this now. Serve the ball and we'll put them away. We've got the advantage."

I nod and remember to breathe. I look into the crowd to find Ryan and my crew, but all I see is Coach K with a satisfied smirk on her face.

I'll show her.

I catch the ball and begin my routine. I bounce the ball off my hand and then on the court. Tossing the ball into the air, I serve it with all my might. "Hee!"

This time the ball lands just wide.

"Out!" the official says.

Minka and Lauren nod to each other and smile. "That's right," Lauren says with a pinch of arrogance. "She always misses her first serve and she can barely get the second one in either," she continues, referring to me.

No!

"40–30," the chair umpire announces. "Match point."

I wipe my eyes, pretending the tear is just sweat.

Bella turns from her spot at mid-court. "Come on, Maggie. It's all good. Don't be me—don't overthink. Just hit the ball."

"Don't think," I say to myself. Don't think about how many points we've lost this season because of my serves.

Don't go there. Just serve.

I bend over and bounce the ball. Then I toss it high into the air. "Hee!" I whip my racquet and smack the ball. My stomach drops. The ball hits the tape and rolls in front of Minka. She swats it with her racquet, pushing the ball to the side.

"Let!" the official calls.

Oh my God. I can feel the eyes of everyone in the complex on me. This is the final. No one should be in the final if they can't even serve. This is so humiliating.

Bella comes over to me again. She takes my shoulders gently and looks into my eyes. "Come on, Maggie. No pressure. We made it this far. Just have fun. That's what counts." She gives me a smile and a squeeze and jogs back to her spot.

Bella telling me to have fun. The irony.

"Deep breath, Mags! You're a beast." Joe shouts.

I'm almost giggling to myself as I bounce the ball. I switch up my routine and bounce one off my elbow and then my knee.

Just have fun.

I grin at Bella when she turns around to check on me. I mouth, "watch this" just like I did the first time Coach K spotted us.

She returns my smile.

I toss the ball in the air and for a moment time stands still. The pressure after double-faulting is intense. *Do I throw in a topspin? Should I go with a high percentage shot? What will they be expecting?* Whatever I do, I can't get into a second serve situation again. The ball drops and I whack it with my racquet. As soon as I make contact, the game resumes in real time. The ball bullets over the net and bounces hard in the box.

Lauren lunges toward it, but she's too late.

"No!" Minka wails as Bella falls on top of me.

"Game! Match!" the official calls out.

"We did it!" Bella yells. Her tears soak my shirt.

The intense stinging of my ripped up knees and elbows fades, replaced with pure joy. My first ace!

Chapter Thirty-Two
BELLA

A little while later, Maggie and I are still celebrating. Ryan, Joe, and a ton of reporters have joined us.

"How does it feel to win against the number one seed?" a guy in a collared shirt asks, shoving a recorder in front of me. Joe steps to the side to allow Maggie and me to soak in our win.

"Is Coach Kasinski responsible for your success?" another reporter asks.

"Maggie, how long have you been playing tennis?"

I smile and begin to answer questions. Maggie stays quiet. And I'm okay with that. We both have our strengths and being the voice of our doubles team is one of mine.

Out of habit, I look around for Coach as I'm answering questions. She's set up her own mini press conference with Lauren, who now has a compression bandage and ice wrapped around her thigh—as if that's what kept the O'Donnells from winning. But I know better. The look on Minka's face, scowling and splotchy with rage, tells me she knows too.

Surprisingly enough, Lauren's boyfriend Brandon is nowhere to be found, but I guess that shouldn't be too surprising . . . Lauren does a good job of keeping him hidden from Coach whenever possible. It's all part of her game. Kind of the opposite approach from Maggie.

Coach is talking loud enough that I can overhear snippets. "Yes," she says at one point. "I saw Bella and Maggie's talent from the moment I met them. In fact, I can't wait to see what they do during the final league matches for Beachwood."

Are you kidding me? She's still trying to take the credit? But I guess this means we're still on the team. She can't kick us off now.

"Congratulations, girls!" Mom and Dad push through the reporters. They both wrap their arms around us, pulling us into a big, sloppy family group hug.

Click. Click. Click.

Cameras flash as the press attempts to capture the moment.

"I always knew you could do it," Mom says to me. Tears stain her cheeks. "I'm so proud of both of you." She looks at Maggie.

Maggie bites her bottom lip and stares at her Nikes.

"Mom, Dad. We need to talk," I say.

My mom and dad look at each other. "That sounds a bit serious, given the occasion," Mom says.

"Right now?" Dad asks.

"Yeah. Now."

I walk Mom, Dad, and Maggie over to the side and away from the hoopla. "Look," I say to my parents. A couple of journalists approach us and I wave them off. "Can you just give me a moment?" I hold up my finger politely.

They look at each other, shrug, and head over to the tent and Coach K.

I turn my attention back to my family. "Maggie and I had a talk about tennis before the match."

Mom pulls out her iPhone. "When do you want to start new lessons? We should really get Joe over here. Joe!"

"Wait." I cut off my mom. "We weren't talking about schedules; we were talking about what we really want to do." I take a deep breath. Maggie chews her lip. "If, and I mean *if*, Maggie and I decide to continue playing—"

"What?" Dad and Mom say at the same time.

I hold up my finger to silence them. "I said, *if* we keep playing, there will need to be some new rules."

Mom places her hand on her hip. "New rules? What on earth are you talking about? Teenage girls don't usually get to set the rules in my house," she says.

"Just hear us out. Rule one: no casting us in roles. Maggie isn't a flake and I'm not perfect, so you need to treat us equally."

Maggie looks up and smiles. She stops chewing on her lip.

Mom and Dad look at each other. Dad shakes his head and runs his fingers through his thinning black hair. Mom rolls her eyes. "We don't—"

"And rule two"—I cut her off—"Maggie and I will be allowed to participate in other activities besides tennis."

"But . . ." Dad says. "What about—"

"And?" Mom asks.

I look to Maggie, who nods. "We get the freedom to decide what to participate in. Or we don't play anymore."

"Wait . . ." Mom says.

"Those are the conditions," I say forcefully.

"Bella, this is a bit of a shock. You never told us you cared so much about doing other activities. We had no idea you felt this way," Dad says, holding out his arms toward Maggie and me.

"Neither did I until recently," I say, beaming at my sister. "Maggie made me see that life isn't an either/or. It's a buffet."

"You know we love both of you more than anything in the world." Mom ruffles our ponytails. "We just want you to be happy," she says, clearing her throat.

"What your mother means is that however you want to handle all this, we'll support you 150 percent." He pats us each on the head. "So do you want to start your lessons with Joe?"

Mom and Dad look around for Joe. When they spot him helping to set up the trophy presentation in the white tent, they charge toward him.

Maggie and I look at each other, roll our eyes, and giggle. "That's probably the best we could have hoped for from them," she says.

"Yeah, but I guess we'll probably have to tell them that this was our last big tournament for a while?"

"Baby steps." She shrugs.

"I don't know. Maybe we should just get it over with after they're done talking to Joe."

"You are fearless," Maggie says, wrapping her arm around my shoulders. Reporters surround us again instantly.

"And so are you," I whisper.

"What do you two think of Coach Kasinski's resignation?" A man with a baseball cap shoves a microphone in front of me.

"Wait." I shake my head, thinking that I must not have heard him correctly. "What did you say?"

"Did you know she plans to take a sabbatical before coaching college tennis next season?" another journalist asks.

I look at Maggie, who shrugs. "We didn't realize that."

"How about the O'Donnells' announcement that they'll be concentrating solely on USTA tournaments?" the man asks. "Lauren said high school tennis distracts them from 'real' play."

Maggie opens her mouth. "Ha! What a load of—"

"Trophy time!" Joe shouts from the tent.

"Excuse us," I say to the reporters. I take Maggie's arm and we weave our way through the crowd toward Joe.

"Did you hear about Coach K?" Maggie asks Joe breathlessly when we reach him.

"Did you hear Minka and Lauren are playing tournaments only?" I add.

"I might have." Joe has that mischievous smile again. "And I also might be interviewing to be the new Beachwood coach."

"Yes!" Maggie shouts. "This is the best day ever!"

"Awesome!" I'm smiling so hard my cheeks hurt.

"We're definitely playing next year!" Maggie wraps her arm around my shoulder.

"I'd hope so considering you'll be Beachwood's number one doubles team," Joe says. "Now go get that trophy, Anderson Aces."

Maggie and I step in front of the huge crowd to accept our

award. We hold hands and take a bow just like we did after our picture book presentation.

Maggie looks at me and smiles. Together, we hoist the trophy above us, and I know that for us, this is just the beginning.

Love may mean nothing in tennis, but when it comes to finding out what's important in life, it means everything. We both discovered our true love that day. And at fifteen that's pretty awesome.

ACKNOWLEDGMENTS

First and foremost, thanks bunches to the Pretty Tough readers. Without you, I could not do what I love everyday. Your e-mails, blogs, and Facebook and Twitter posts inspire me each and every day to write sporty books for girls.

This book would not be close to what it is without major assistance from the following people: Jane and George Schonberger, Gillian Levinson, Ben Schrank, Michelle Grajkowski, the amazing professionals at Razorbill, Cory Coffey McGee, Katherine Jennifer Krylova, Katia Rania, and every single person I bugged with tennis and BMX questions. I'm forever grateful for your support.

A special thanks to the tremendously patient Coach Joe at the Cape May Tennis Club for the hours he spent teaching me not only how to play tennis, but also the rules and special insights into the world of this incredible game. Also, thanks to the ladies' group for letting a rookie join in on a few doubles games.

As always, thanks bunches to my family: Mom, Dad, Kelly, Anthony, Nicole, Michael, Ida, Ron, Sydney, and Sabrina. I'm so blessed to be surrounded by such support and love. Also, a huge thanks to my tribe. Justin, I would never have time to write a word without your endless assistance. Kaci Olivia, your authentic self is always my inspiration. I love you both bunches.

And last, but certainly not least, God, thank you for all my blessings, including our newest arrival, due to make his or her debut after the publication of this novel.